A Merry Chatty Christmas

Also by Ronda Rich

Saint Simons Island
A Stella Bankwell Mystery
(The first in the series)

Sapelo Island
(Second in the Stella Bankwell series)

What Southern Women Know (That Every Woman Should)

My Life in The Pits: A NASCAR Memoir

What Southern Women Know about Flirting

What Southern Women Know about Faith

The Town that Came A-Courtin' (a novel and television movie)

There's A Better Day A-Comin'

Mark My Words: A Memoir of Mama

Let Me Tell You Something

RONDA RICH

A Merry Chatty Christmas

A Stella Bankwell Story

MERCER UNIVERSITY PRESS
Macon, Georgia

MUP/H1055

Published by Mercer University Press
1501 Mercer University Drive
Macon, Georgia 31207

29 28 27 26 25 5 4 3 2 1

Books published by Mercer University Press are printed on acid-free paper that meets the requirements of the American National Standard for Information Sciences—Permanence of Paper for Printed Library Materials.

Printed and bound in CANADA.

This book is set in Adobe Garamond.

Cover/jacket design by Burt&Burt.

ISBN (Print) 978-088146-981-3
ISBN (eBook) 978-088146-982-0

Cataloging-in-Publication Data is available from the Library of Congress

It is only right to dedicate this book to late U.S. Senator, Governor, and Lt. Governor for sixteen years of the State of Georgia. Zell Miller is my McCager Burnett: crusty, tough, smart, and completely dedicated to the people of the mountains. He was my mentor. I was his Stella. "Girl, let me tell you something: don't ever leave your mountain people behind. That's who you are." I hope I have done him rightly proud with Stella Bankwell.

And to Mrs. Shirley (Zell) Miller who has picked up where his death forced him to stop. She is Alva Burnett in every way: Always supportive of her husband and loving and kind to everyone. As he would say: She was his biggest asset.

I thank God for putting these two people in my life.

Chapter One

Stella Bankwell was in the cheeriest of moods, one that had just brightened more because she had taken an exit off a four-lane, headed to the two-lane country road where her idea of heaven was waiting about fifty miles away.

As she passed through the town, she smiled at the Christmas decorations that lit up the early darkness of the winter's evening. The trees in the center of the town's square, wrapped from the ground to the sky with white lights, sparkled like diamonds. A twenty-foot tall holly bush, trimmed to a point at the top, glistened with the old-fashioned big-bulbed lights in red, green, and blue.

On the roof of a hardware store were five-foot tall letters glowing in red that said, "Jesus Is The Reason." Next to it was a Christmas tree lot where families, bundled up against the cold, were shopping for a last-minute tree. The holiday abounded all around with trees decorated on lawns, and every business glistened with beautiful decorations. Stella, stopped at a traffic light, looked at it and couldn't help but grin.

"I'll be home for Christmas," she sang softly.

The traffic light changed, and she gently pressed the gas pedal driving slowly down historic Green Street, where Antebellum and turn-of-the-century homes with enormous columns and balconies were so dressed up that the decorations and lights stunned her with their beauty.

Wishing to absorb more of the wonderland, she turned into the drive of one of the houses with a law office sign in front. The little girl in Stella came rushing back as she recalled the happy Christmases of her growing-up years. But back then, no one had an abundance of lights or boughs loaded with Christmas balls and strands of mistletoe.

She laid her head back against the seat and pondered on those mountain Christmases of her youth when she and her sister, Lynn, would tramp through the woods on their farm, searching for the perfect tree. Both would complain that, out of one hundred acres of wooded land, it was hard to find the right size tree that wasn't too thin on one side or too thick for hanging ornaments.

An additional seventy-five acres were set aside for the farming their daddy did, aided by his helper, Rooster, and his teenage son, Bubba, who worked after school and on Saturdays. On Sundays, they laid down their work, picked up their Bibles, and headed to church. No work on the Lord's Day. It was a hard farming life a good bit of the time when the winters were too cold and the summers too dry to give them at least two cuttings of hay. The perfect summer, rare though it was, gave them three cuttings of hay.

Sims Jackson, though, was not a man to shy away from hard work. He was up before dawn as soon as he smelled that his wife, Martha Annie, was frying sausage or bacon while making biscuits and gravy. She made certain that he had a hearty breakfast before heading out for a day where he would half-walk/half-run from task to task. Dinner, what the country folks called it, is what the city folks call lunch, was equally hearty where she served a hot meal for Sims and Rooster and, on Saturdays, for Bubba, too.

Bubba, a shy, nice-looking, blondish-headed boy, had a crush on Lynn, so, once the girls found the right Christmas tree, he was proud to be asked to cut it down and bring it back to the two-story, white clapboard farmhouse that was shaded by two hearty oak trees and a smaller maple at the backdoor.

"Big enough that I need to take the tractor to pull it in?" he'd always ask. Lynn, who should have been ashamed by how she led the poor boy on all the time when her heart was set on Ronnie, batted her lashes and put a hand on his forearm.

"Why, Bubba, as strong as you are, you don't need a tractor." She smiled beguilingly. "But why don't you take it and a chain? I don't want to overtire you. You've already worked so hard today."

Stella would turn her back and roll her eyes. Every year, the same spiel. That is, until the year that the eighteen-year-old Lynn had slipped up and called him "Ronnie" instead of "Bubba." From then on, until the girls finished college, Bubba would not be lured flirtatiously by Lynn. He would only bring the tree in if Stella, always the same sweet girl, would ask him. To be truthful, though Lynn was quite pretty, with glistening long brown hair and large brown eyes, it was Stella who was slowly changing from a redheaded, freckled faced, pigtailed girl into a breathtaking beauty. Her senior year, classmates had unanimously voted her "Most Beautiful" while Lynn's senior classed voted her—in a tie with Selma Moses—"Biggest Flirt".

Stella closed her eyes, and a string of memories danced across her mind: putting the tree up no later than December 10th while playing Christmas carols on the record player and sipping spiced tea made with cinnamon, cloves, tea, and sugar. When Mawmaw Jackson was alive, she always brought over her special teacakes. Sims, worn out from another hard day, fell asleep in his chair while reading the newspaper as his girls made merriment with their decorating.

Sims Jackson. The most honorable man in several counties was Stella's hero. The thought of him brought a glisten of tears. She shook herself out of the moment and took one long, last look at the beauty of the antique houses and the street that shined brighter than the stars in the sky. She pulled her car to the back parking lot, turned the big SUV around, then drove out onto the magnificent street and headed north toward home.

She was still wrapped tightly in nostalgia and magic, enjoying every minute of it, when the phone rang. She hit the button on the steering wheel.

"Stella Faye!" squealed Chatty. "For the life of me, I will never understand how someone I adore could completely treat me so disgracefully."

In the flash of those few seconds, Stella's magical feeling evaporated like water poured on a sizzling July sidewalk. Chatham Balsam Colquitt IV was her best friend. They both knew she loved him deeply because no one else could charm her, chastise her, or make her madder than he.

Stella tried to adjust to the sudden switch of emotion, but anger began to rise up from the pit of her stomach. Or, at the very least, annoyance.

"Chatty, what is it this time?" she asked with indisputable irritation. Though she really felt the emotion, she was faking the intensity. She knew when she spoke to Chatty like that, it rattled him. He was accustomed to people who bowed to him. Stella and McCager Burnett, the former governor of Georgia who, with his wife, Alva, thought of Chatty as a son, were the only ones who could keep him in line. Somewhat. When his parents died and left "Chatham" as they called him, with more wealth than he could ever spend, as well as two mansions and a South Georgia plantation, McCager, an estate attorney, was the executor of their will. He took the sad, lost teenager under their wings of love and care and were grateful for the opportunity since they had never been blessed with the children they so desired.

Taken aback and feigning hurt, he paused before replying, "What is wrong with my sweet Stellie? Where did she go? She has been replaced by someone of tremendous unkindness. Please, bring my Stellie back. I love her so."

While he spoke, Stella pulled onto Route 129, the highway that would take her straight to Turner's Corner and her family's farm. In addition to rolling her eyes, she sighed.

"Hellooooo," Chatty chirped, "Are you there?"

"Chatham, you have called me eight or nine times in less than an hour. I'm trying to enjoy the evening before Christmas Eve. Silent night, you know?"

"Well." He answered in a clipped tone. "Spencer, my devoted butler, and I shall just carry on and IF we ever get to the hinterlands wherein there lays your family farm, I shall dial the home phone and alert your sainted mother." His spunk was returning. "But I'll tell you one thing, Stella Faye Jackson Bankwell, Joseph and Mary got to Bethlehem on a DONKEY faster than we are getting to your farm in an extremely high-dollar vehicle. Good. Bye."

He was gone. For the moment. He'd be back before she could get to Turner's Corner. Stella, stubborn redhead that she was, determined that she would regain her joyous mood. Leaving town with its lovely lights behind her, she passed many houses all decked out in

Christmas cheer. One house had its roof covered in lights with an inflatable snowman and Santa Claus on each side of its red foiled front door. Another house—an updated mid-century covered in white paint—displayed its tree in the large plate glass window in the front.

Stella smiled. When she was growing up, people always placed their trees in their front window so they could be admired as folks drove by. Stella's family did it, too, but it mattered little. They lived off a rural road not traveled much, especially since the Jacksons owned most of the land on one side of the road and twenty acres on the other side. Then, to get to the farmhouse, it required traveling an 800-foot long, dusty driveway. But the visitors who saw it, always bragged on Lynn and Stella's decorating skills and the perfection with which they strategically placed the tinsel on the tree.

"Oh, tinsel, I kinda miss it," Stella sighed. She was starting to return to cheeriness. "Silver bells, silver bells, it's Christmas time in the mountains," she adlibbed as she sang. "Wait a minute! Why am I singing this to myself when I have a wonderful CD." Stella always talked aloud to herself when she was in the car alone. Everyone teased her endlessly about it. Even sometimes when she was a passenger, she'd be internally dialoguing and making the expressions to match.

"It keeps me sane," she had once remarked to her close friend, Marlo, who thought it was the craziest thing she'd ever seen. It always annoyed Asher, her ex-husband.

She reached into the console beside her and pulled out her favorite Christmas CD, *Christmas by the Isaacs*. The bluegrass/gospel group was her favorite, especially when she wanted to be reminded of the mountains. The blood harmony of the family's voices, the upright bass, guitars and mandolin were sometimes the medicine she needed if she got homesick on St. Simons Island where she now lived because of Asher Bankwell. She pushed that messy marriage out of her mind, but smiled when she wondered if anyone had sent a fruitcake to Asher in federal prison. She couldn't help it. She had to laugh out loud at the thought.

"Asher," she said, popping the CD cover open by pressing it against her thigh and flipping the top up with her thumbnail. "It's a long way from those black tie, over-the-top, Christmas Eve parties we used to give in our Atlanta Buckhead mansion to an orange jumpsuit and a bare prison cell." Then, sweetly, she added, "Maybe they'll give you and your concubine, Annabelle, an extra pack of peanuts from Santa." She chuckled again.

She pushed the disc in, hit play, and the Isaacs' family harmony filled the car with the sounds of "Winter Wonderland." Peacefully, she sighed and thought of her Mama, just forty-five minutes away. She knew that Mama was in the kitchen and that there would be her homemade four-layer coconut cake waiting as well as Mama's much-beloved chocolate cake with a seven-minute icing.

Recovered completely from Chatty's constant annoyance, she was passing through the little community of Quillian's Corner with a hardware store, tiny grocery store, a bank, and a pharmacy. She was driving by Wauka Mountain Pharmacy, admiring the lights dangling from its long, wide window when her phone rang. She tried to steel herself against aggravation toward Chatty for another stupid question like the one three calls ago. "Does your mother possess a large silver chafing dish? Spencer packed two but I fear dreadfully that we may require three for Christmas dinner."

"Chatty, you know good and well that my family has no silver. No one in Turner's Corner has any silver. Unless it's a silver half-dollar." Chatty had insisted on packing up his best china, which he had imported directly from Wedgewood in England after flying over there to select it, antique crystal tea glasses, and enough silver serving pieces to line the length of the Jackson farmhouse. And, as if that was not enough, he was bringing along his British butler, Spencer—his Atlanta butler—because Bailey was his butler on Sea Island. Spencer, extraordinarily well-trained, had served the Royal household in London. Once he saw Turner's Corner, he might grab his passport and head back to England. For the entire five-hour drive, Chatty had called Stella with such nonsense. He had also packed up stunning Christmas decorations purchased from McElhaney's, the most exclusive shop in Buckhead, where only the rich locals shopped.

"Just in case," he had said, eyeing her knowingly the previous evening when she had spent the night in his guesthouse. She took a gulp of wine and said nothing.

The Isaacs were now singing "It's Christmas Time Again" when a feeling of absolute ugliness swept over her. Why had she ever thought it was a good idea to invite Chatty for Christmas? Momentarily, she forgot how much she cherished him and how she couldn't bear the thought of him being alone for Christmas. Since after she and Asher divorced, there was no place for Chatty to be on Christmas Eve. No more black tie or ridiculously expensive Christmas Eve parties. During their marriage, Chatty invited them to his stunning mansion for brunch on Christmas Day. That's why she invited him. That and because he had been a steadfast, loving friend to her. But, as the phone rang again, all that escaped her.

She punched the button on the steering wheel with much more force than necessary.

"WHAT?!?" She practically screamed in a tone much too mean for the person the much beloved Stella really was. "I thought I told you to stop calling every few minutes!"

"Stella?" asked a man with a beautiful Southern drawl. His tone was quizzical.

Like an inflatable Santa Claus that had been knifed with a pair of kitchen scissors, she completely deflated, then hit the steering wheel with her fist, mad at herself.

"Oh, Pepper, hi," she said meekly.

Her stomach took a sickening roll. The most wonderful, incredibly handsome man she knew had just seen the worst side of Stella Bankwell.

Perhaps this wasn't going to be such a joyful Christmas after all.

Chapter Two

Stella, mighty embarrassed by the way she had just answered the phone, was on the brink of tears. Were she to admit it to herself, she always wanted US Marshal Jackson Culpepper to see her in the best of light. The truth of the matter was that she rarely let her guard down unless it was with Chatty, and everyone who knew Chatty, understood why. He meant well, especially with Stella, but sometimes it came across in an irritating manner.

"Uh, Pepper, I was, uh," she was stuttering. If only she had thought to tell the truth because there was no need to hide it or be embarrassed.

Pepper started laughing. "Oh, Stella, no need for apology. Our friendship is too deep for that." He chuckled again in a knowing way. "Let me take one guess why the sweetest girl I know is in such a foul mood. Does it happen to have anything to do with Mr. Chatham Balsam Colquitt IV?"

Relief swept over her. Of course, Pepper, law officer that he was, could quickly assess a situation, especially one he knew so well. Stella, Pepper, Chatty and McCager Burnett had solved two recent crimes together, and Miss Alva, McCager's wife, had even helped out on their last adventure on Sapelo Island. In the course of the last year or so, the original four had become increasingly close. Stella, Chatty, and the Burnetts were already family, but Pepper, who was working at the United States Marshal training facility, Glynco, in Brunswick, had proven himself worthy of being an extended member of their foursome. They all had a great deal of respect and love for each other even though Pepper was relatively new to the friends who had known one another for much of their lives.

Stella sighed. "Of course, it does. I spent the night in his guest house last night, to cut up the travel, plus I wanted to see a couple of friends for lunch. I spent the afternoon shopping at Phipps. I adore St. Simons and my precious cottage, but I do have to admit that I miss Buckhead sometimes and the excitement of Phipps. Particularly at Christmas. However, I realized that I do not miss the traffic which is why it's 6:30 and I'm still more than an hour away from Mama's."

"Did you and Chatty have one of your well-known skirmishes this morning?"

"No, although I did tell him that it was not necessary to bring his Porthault sheets, silver, and his English butler." Stella explained how Chatty had been calling every few minutes with ridiculous questions. "For instance, they were so busy packing up his mansion that they got a later start than I did. He left behind the *priceless* gravy bowl that once belonged to Queen Victoria so he called to say he was having a 'spell' over it." She stopped to allow Pepper to laugh so hard, he choked and had to take a few sips of water. "Of course, he quickly blamed it on poor Spencer who endures so much." She paused to think for a moment before asking her question. "Do you think I was wrong in asking him to Christmas? I don't want to make an aggravation for Mama."

"Not at all," Pepper replied immediately. "Chatty needs you and the Burnetts. He pretends that his great fortune fulfills his every need but, deep down, he's lonely. You know, Stella, I've been around long enough to believe that if Chatty had to make a choice between his mansions and you, he'd pick you."

"Ha!" Stella scoffed cynically. "We'll have to pry stock certificates out of his dying hands. Besides, I'll be gone to meet the good Lord long before Chatty. He has such a life of leisure that he'll live to be a hundred and twenty."

The marshal was no fool. He knew better. Growing up in Memphis, his own mama used to say that she had never seen a boy with such instincts and intuition. Once, a man had moved two houses up from the Culpeppers' on their pretty tree-lined street that was just inside the city limits. Pepper was nine and was playing sidewalk hopscotch with two friends between the houses. The new neighbor sauntered by, stopped and watched the boys for a time, then offered a quarter to whoever could win a game of jacks.

Pepper's reflexes were unbeatable. When he was training at Glynco, he was the top shooter in the class and the quickest draw. He easily won the jacks to the disappointment of his two friends, each who had been hoping for an ice cream cone.

"You're pretty good there, son," the man named Melvin McComb remarked as he reached into his pocket for a quarter. Pepper stood up and, just like his father had drilled into him, he extended his hand, looked him straight in the eye and said, "I'm Jackson Culpepper."

Mr. McComb, quite impressed, shook hands and said, "It's nice to meet such a fine, Southern gentleman." A shorty, pudgy, middle-aged man, he bowed to the little boy. He straightened up and looked Pepper right in the eye, which was the beginning of the troubles for Mr. McComb. Pepper tilted his head, studied him for a moment, thanked him for the quarter, then scooped up his jacks, hollered goodbye to his friends and hurried home. He ran up the steps of the Culpeppers' turn-of-the century, Victorian house with its wraparound porch that had been built by his great-grandfather. He flung the door open and, even though his mama had reprimanded him many times about entering the home in a peaceful way, he slammed the door, shouting for his mother.

"Mom! Mom!" he called in an urgent tone.

Sarah Culpepper appeared at the top of the stairs then, seeing her son, ran down the steps. "Pep! What's wrong? Have you been hurt?" She could see he was trembling so she sat down on the second step from the bottom and pulled him into her arms.

"Son, what's the matter? Why are you so upset?" He was breathing in heaves.

"Mom, you know the man that moved into Mrs. Henson's house?"

"Yes, your father went down and welcomed him to the neighborhood and I sent him a pecan pie."

"Something's wrong. I got a real bad feelin' about him. He just gave me a quarter for winning a game of jacks against Colton and Mike. I shook his hand like dad taught me. But when I looked into his eyes, I felt evil. I ain't never felt that way before. He scared me real bad."

His mother held him tightly until he had stopped shaking. "Let's go in the kitchen for a glass of milk and chocolate chip cookies I made this afternoon."

He took a sip of milk and nibbled on a cookie. He had no appetite. Sarah Culpepper leaned against the kitchen counter, arms folded, and studied her son. She was certain that something was really wrong. She called her husband at his office and he came home immediately. That was his parents' first encounter with the remarkable intuition of their son. McComb, as it turned out, was wanted for first degree murder for killing a store clerk during a robbery. He had been too smart to use his real name, but the law, nonetheless, figured it out after a couple of days of investigation. Sarah's cousin was a Memphis police investigator. He knew what a sensible boy Pepper was and he trusted him.

Over the years, the family would laugh and recall the first criminal that Pepper, at the age of nine, had collared. It helped push him more assuredly into a career as a lawman. He was proud of himself and grateful for the opportunities he had been given and the mentors who invested in him. He had worked hard as a marshal, though he had, at one time, considered joining the Secret Service. Growing up, however, he loved reruns of *Gunsmoke* and was starry-eyed about Marshal Matt Dillon, so that settled it—Jackson Culpepper became a US Marshal and a much awarded, respected one.

Pepper laughed again. The interaction between Stella and Chatty was the most relaxing entertainment he ever seemed to get aside from target shooting.

"Trust me, Stella Bankwell. He worships the ground you walk on." She was starting to soften. She couldn't stay mad at Chatty for too long.

"Well, honestly, Pepper, one call was asking where the nearest liquor store was in the harrowing event that he might need to purchase additional champagne. First of all, we live in a dry county. Second, we're thirty miles from the nearest grocery store. He's been to our farm before. He knows we're simple mountain people. This certainly won't be a shock to his delicate system. My mama, for some reason, pets him and makes over him like he's a lovable puppy. Which just makes him worse. She usually defends him against me."

"Stella, I have a feeling that this is going to be Mr. Colquitt's most wondrous Christmas. I can feel it in my gut. How far before you're home?"

"Another twenty miles, I just got to Cleveland. You're still coming up, aren't you?" She held her hand up to nervously finger the collar of her shirt. She hadn't mentioned to him or anyone that she'd be crushed if he had changed his mind or work kept him away. She wanted to spend Christmas with him.

"You betcha. I never miss any invitation to watch you and Chatty banter," he replied light-heartedly. "I really appreciate the Burnetts inviting me to their farm for Christmas, especially since I only have two days off and couldn't get to Memphis. How far is it between your farm and theirs?"

"Oh, a mile or so, and part of that is our long driveway. I've walked over there plenty of times. In fact, the farm which Miss Alva inherited from her daddy used to adjoin our land. But I heard tell that her daddy had fallen on some hard times, when her mama got sick and there were a lot of medical bills to pay, so he sold off about fifteen acres between us. That was back in the days when country folks didn't have insurance. Daddy said if he had known they were selling it, he would have bought it. Mama said that it sold again about a year ago to a couple in their thirties. She is, in biblical terms, 'with child.' Mama said they had wanted a baby so much and have waited for years. They're very excited." She giggled. "I always tell more to the story than I'm sure a lawman wants to hear."

He closed his eyes and thought he was smelling her sweet perfume. The sound of her voice almost made him swoon. Which he might have done if he hadn't been a tough marshal. Or rather, was supposed to be a tough marshal. Stella had a way of melting him like a roasted marshmallow. He thought Stella might reciprocate his feelings, but he wasn't sure and he was too proud to show his cards first. He told himself that, apparently, his remarkable instincts did not work with women, especially beautiful Southern belles, particularly Stella Bankwell.

"Stella, I love your stories. I do have to run right now because I need to finish some paperwork. I had to stop in Atlanta to bring in some original copies with signatures. I'm gonna stay here for the night then head out about seven. I don't want to get there too early and bother the Burnetts." A small laugh. Stella loved all his various laughs and chuckles. "With Atlanta traffic, you never can tell when I'll be there. But rest assured, I'll be there in time to watch the majority of your and Chatty's escapades."

"Try to be there for a late breakfast. We'll wait until 10:30. You must have Mama's biscuits and gravy with bacon, eggs, and cheese grits. You might know Southern cooking but wait until you taste Appalachian cooking."

"I'll dream about it all night," he replied—yet thinking it would be Stella in his dreams, not biscuits and gravy. "I'll call you when I'm about halfway there. Should I stop at the Burnetts, first?"

"Mama already called and invited them. We'll have the whole family together. Just give me a call. Cell service isn't great there, so I'll text you the number of Mama's landline."

"I can't wait. Be careful. Remember, there are a lot of deer out, just waiting to hit a car. Keep your eyes peeled. Looking forward to seeing you tomorrow."

She paused a second. "I'm so glad you're joining us for Christmas."

"That makes two of us."

The moment that Stella hit the button to end the call as she was crossing the bridge over the Tesnatee Creek, the phone rang again. This time, Stella let it ring long enough for the caller I.D. to flash on the screen. She rolled her eyes.

She answered, pushing a smile in her voice. "My darlin' Chatty. It's been so long since we talked. TWENTY minutes."

His heart melted. Stella and the Burnetts were all the family he had. This, he believed, was going to be the best Christmas he'd had since he was a child.

"Stella, love, will your mother mind that I didn't bring my black tie attire? I brought a black suit and tie."

She was passing Tesnatee Baptist Church and Camp Barney, next door. Her heart was swelling with anticipation of home, that precious place that had raised her.

"Stella? Are you there?"

"Chatty, I think you might be a bit overdressed. Do you own a pair of jeans?"

He gasped. "Jeans?? Gentlemen of refinement do not wear jeans. My finely-manicured hands have never touched a pair."

"Well, okay, Mr. Refinement, Mama and I'll wait supper on you and Spencer."

She clicked off the phone, grateful that McCager Burnett would be there to keep Chatty in line as best as possible. The thought tickled her.

Then she shook head, remembering Chatty's asking about the chafing dish.

Neither of us can understand the upbringing of the other, she thought to herself, *yet our hearts match like two pieces of a puzzle.*

Chapter Three

Stella turned onto the gravel road that was actually the drive to their farm. On both sides of the road were hay fields where she had often helped her daddy, Rooster, and Bubba get up hay.

She stopped the car for a moment and remembered the sizzling hot summer days and how hard they worked. She'd drive one of the farm's old trucks—no air conditioning or radio and a gear shifter that frequently stuck—following behind her daddy, Sims Jackson, and his tractor as it baled the cut hay. Bubba, his green John Deere-billed hat soaked with sweat, followed, tossing the bales onto the back of the truck.

That 1957 GMC with wood rails, still stored in one of their barns, could be downright hateful. Sometimes, Bubba would holler for her to stop so he could step up on the tailgate and toss in a couple more square bales. Sitting on the tailgate, he'd call, "Let's head for the barn." With the clutch pushed to the floor, she struggled with both hands to get the truck back in gear. Finally, it would cooperate, and they'd bounce uncomfortably to the barn, unload, and head right on back to the hayfield.

Sims had died from injuries sustained in a tractor accident when she was in college. Rooster was slowing down a lot but he still helped around the farm. And Bubba managed it, raising white-faced registered Angus, selling and buying as needed. Stella's mama would have closed down the farm after Sims died, but Bubba convinced her to keep it going and they would be partners, splitting every cent of profit. Never married, Bubba lived in a small house on the property that had been built for the farm help many years before. Most nights, he and Miss Martha Annie shared supper at her kitchen table.

When Stella felt a lump tug at her throat, she drove on from the hay fields and started to pass through the Georgia pines and maples. Then, she hit the brakes again and put the car in park. She couldn't believe what she was seeing.

"Oh, my!" Stella put her hand on her heart as tears welled up. It was the old, black 1957 pick-up, outlined in old-fashioned Christmas lights, burning brightly, three pieces of wood nailed together, then painted with red lettering, and sprigs of live holly stuck to it.

"Merry Christmas," read the sign outlined with smaller lights.

In the truck bed were three square bales of hay, which built a triangle, holding another sign. This one with green lettering: "Welcome HOME, Stella."

She jumped out of the car and ran over to see it closer. It was prettier than anything she had ever seen at Phipps Plaza. She snapped several photos, one selfie (though she normally hated them) and walked around the masterpiece. At the back, under the opened tailgate, was a gas generator powering the lights. She didn't think that anything could make coming home any sweeter, but this certainly did. She and her old friend, the ancient truck, spent several minutes together, then she gently patted the hood. "You ornery old thing. I still love ya'." Stella smiled and walked away until she couldn't help but look back. What a precious homecoming gift.

She put the car in drive and looked across the hayfield to her right where she could see lamps and ceiling lights glowing over at the Burnetts. A trail of smoke drifted up from the chimney. McCager Burnett loved sitting by that fireplace in the old farmhouse. That was his reading place. Always at night, he'd read the Bible by rocking in a comfortable, perfectly-cushioned chair, then he would turn his attention to a book of nonfiction, normally historical. Miss Alva generally sat on the other side of the fireplace, either reading or doing needlepoint.

Stella sighed. Home. And all the people she loved. Fifty feet into the tunnel created by the tall pines, she saw the weathered, gray sign that said: Piney Wood Farm. As always, her mama had affixed a big red bow to it. Ahead on the right, sat the two-story farmhouse that needed a new coat of paint. But it was cheerful with a wreath on the front door, red cushions on the porch swing, and two rocking chairs. And the best part:

the Christmas tree shining colorfully in the front window. Stella couldn't help herself, she had to take another stop and look. She thought about what her daddy had said when she left for college.

"Baby girl, good Lord willin', you'll be back to visit but you won't return to live here." Sims' eyes watered. "Them days are done gone. But if trouble or sadness comes your way—and I pray it won't—you're always welcomed home. One day, though, after you've been out in a different world, you'll come back and you'll see this old home place with different eyes. Trust me on that. You'll even long for days that used to be, the days you're runnin' away from now." He sniffed back the tears then hugged her. "Your mama and me, we're mighty proud of you. We love ya." He took her chin in his hand then smiled and winked.

As she looked appreciatively at home, she realized what he'd meant that day and how true it was. She looked upward and whispered. "I love you, Daddy." What had ever made her think that she belonged in Atlanta's high society where everyone competed to have the best and newest? In the beginning, she was so smitten with Asher Bankwell that she thought that she, a square peg, could fit into a round hole. Of course, they all pretended she was welcome and as much a part of their society as if she had been born a blue blood rather than just marrying one. She enjoyed it for a time. She loved the Ansley Park mansion, the Mercedes convertible, and the money to buy the newest fashions by the hottest designers. At the time, it felt good. And right.

But as her grandmother would have said, had she lived to see Stella as such—and thank goodness she didn't—"Why, girl, you's just a country hog a-tryin' to citify yournself with a fancy set of pearls. Be proud of where you come from. We's just as good as them. Least ways in the good Lord's eyes, we is."

Those days were well past, and Asher would be spending the next 20 years in federal prison for his misdeeds. The old farmhouse she was looking at now was far more beautiful to her than the Ansley Park mansion had ever been. She'd had to go away to understand how meaningful this farm was to her. As usual, Sims Jackson had been right.

She gently eased the car over the simple wooden bridge which crossed the brook that ran through the front yard and pulled up to the kitchen door. She stepped out again, into the stinging cold air that she'd not noticed when she'd stopped at the old farm truck. Her mama flung open the kitchen door, smiling from ear to ear. As usual, she was wearing an apron, her favorite one—blue and white gingham check with a pocket whose stitching had come undone at one corner. She was medium height, around ten pounds heavier than pleased her doctor, and her gray hair was cut just below her ears and naturally curled up, attractively. She was a pleasant, nice-looking woman, beloved by her church and community. This did not mean, though, that she let her daughters get by with anything.

She still ran a tight ship and spoke her mind wherever she thought necessary.

Once, when Stella was in high school, a date, Neal O'Kelley, came by to pick her up. Stella, the prettiest girl in school, with long golden-red hair, eyes the color of green velvet, and stunning legs, came bouncing down the steps when her mama called up that Neal had arrived. Stella was wearing a short dress—one her mama had made but which Stella had re-hemmed to a shorter length—and knee-high boots.

Martha Annie Jackson's mouth dropped. She was stumped for a moment then said, "If you were gonna wear a dress up to your tail, why didn't you just wear a bathin' suit?"

It embarrassed Stella beyond imagination. The next morning at breakfast, Stella, still peeved, asked, "Mama, how could you say that in front of Neal? He'll never ask me out again. Couldn't you have waited and straightened me out this morning?"

Martha Annie didn't look up from the gravy she was stirring in her favorite cast iron skillet. "I had to say it then. Otherwise, I might've forgot."

"It embarrassed me to death."

Her mama slid the skillet off the stove. "You done it to yourself, little girl. That'll teach'cha."

They had laughed over that many times since then. Of course, it took years to see the funny in it. That was all in the past. Right now, Mama's baby had come home and all she could think of was happiness.

"Hey, Mama!" Stella called, her warm breath steaming the cold air. She ran to her mama, and they hugged tightly.

"Oh, Stella, it's so good that you're home. Come on in and get out of this cold air. We've got a big snow storm a-comin'."

"Snow? We usually don't get snow here until after Christmas."

"Well, that's what the weatherman and my arthritis say. And my calendar with the signs of the moon, from down at the funeral, home agrees with both of us."

Stella laughed. Nothing felt better than being home. Especially one in the Appalachian foothills.

ଓ

Stella had just finished unloading the car and hanging up her clothes when she heard the kitchen door. The soft sound of voices drifted up the stairs.

"Surely, that's not Chatty. He said he'd call first," Stella said aloud as she finished touching up her make-up, then twisted her long hair up and clasped it. She stepped back to check herself in the mirror, happy she had lost five pounds recently. She smoothed her black dress pants and pulled on a white, beaded, red cardigan over her crisp white shirt. When Chatty was around, she had to look her best to avoid his steely critiques.

The old stairs that led to the living room squeaked as they had for as long as she could remember. It was music to her ears. She walked into the kitchen and saw the back of a lean, long-legged man dressed in jeans, farm boots, a barn coat, and holding a hat in his hands as he talked to her mama. The collar of the coat was flipped up, around a bounty of light blonde hair.

"Stella, look who's here," her mama said as the man turned. He was one of the handsomest men she'd ever seen. He had blue eyes that crinkled as he smiled, a sharp jawline, and a straight, lean nose. He wore a cowboy hat. He said not a word as Stella tilted her head and looked at him. He looked familiar but she couldn't place him. Noticing her puzzlement, he started to laugh, making him even more handsome.

"C'mon, Little Star, you don't remember your buddy?" he asked.

Little Star? Was it? Could it be? Surprise fanned across her face.

"Bubba?" she asked, still searching for more clues. He was so much taller since she last saw him.

He walked toward her, grinning. "Still the prettiest girl around. Got a hug for an old friend?"

They shared a friendly, family-like hug. "Bubba, I would have never known you. I haven't seen you since I left for college."

The kitchen phone rang and Martha Annie answered. "Hello, Chatty! Are you close?" She listened to the answer. As she was directing Chatty to the farm road, Bubba and Stella continued to talk.

"Probably, that's the last you saw of me, but I saw you at your daddy's funeral." His marble blue eyes saddened. "I should've come up and given my sympathy." He swallowed. "I was takin' it real hard. That's why I couldn't be a pallbearer. Not just because I loved him but also because I'm the one who found him." He shook his head and brushed an eye. "Reckon I'll never get over that." He cleared his throat. Stella reached for his left hand and squeezed it. "Kin you ever forgive me?"

"I already have." She hugged him again.

"How is it we ain't seen each other in such a mighty long time?"

She shrugged. "Timing, I suppose. When Asher and I split up, I spent a week here, but you were away at a farming convention. In Nashville, I think."

"Knoxville. But you got the state right." He winked. "Farmin's always been hard, but these days it costs more to feed these cows than we get for 'em at the sale. Still, we're fightin' the good fight. We sell silage and hay. Sometimes, I make a little extra by bush hoggin' for others. That helps me and your mama keep the equipment up. I ain't a-givin' up. We're Appalachian folk. We're tough. Remember when—"

Just then, Bubba was interrupted by the biggest clatter Piney Wood Farm had ever heard echo through a night. Chatham Balsam Colquitt IV had arrived and was loudly directing Spencer as to where the silver flatware was and other commands. Martha Annie went to the back door and called to him.

"Chatty, we're in the kitchen. Come this a-way."

"Spencer, you bring everything in this door. It's too cold for me. I might catch a fever."

Chatty swooped in with all the grandeur he possessed, as though he were entering the Waldorf-Astoria in its grandest days.

"Miss Mama!" he exclaimed happily, taking both of her hands and bowing gallantly.

"Miss Mama?" Bubba mumbled to himself.

"I can just see you in a little deep blue velvet suit and white knee socks when you were four," Stella commented dryly while Bubba stared at the likes of something he had never seen in all his born days.

"My darling Stella!" He spread his arms wide and rushed over to hug her. "I haven't seen you in hours. Feels like *weeks*." After he hugged her, he stepped back and eyed her from her red high heels to her glistening red hair. "Per-fect, darlin'. Just marvelous." He folded his arms over his vast chest which was covered by a tailor-made white shirt, red cashmere sweater, and a navy, double-breasted jacket. "But you know, Stella Faye, I forgot how ragged it looks out here."

Stella closed her eyes and shook her head. Bubba, she was certain, had just been offended—something one never wants to do to a proud Appalachian man.

Chapter Four

It was always challenging to introduce Chatty to Stella's mountain friends. He almost instantly offended someone. When Chatty met her sister Lynn's husband, Ronnie, she was afraid that Ronnie was going to knock Chatty across the room with a right fist to the jaw.

Mountain men still enjoyed a good fistfight and saw no political incorrectness in it. And, of course, no one in Turner's Corner or thereabouts was going to bring a lawsuit. Usually, they just fell out with each other, slugged it out, then forgot it sooner or later. Normally, it was "later" because the Appalachian natives were descendants of the Scotch-Irish who were known for holding grudges that went with them to their graves.

Unfortunately, Ronnie was in a very bad mood the night he met Chatty. Ronnie and Lynn raised thoroughbred horses and one was down mighty sick. The veterinarian was out of town and trying to talk Ronnie through the nursing. A medicine that was needed was out of stock in the three closest towns, but, finally, their vet found a bottle in Blairsville. So, Lynn had driven up the treacherous, winding mountain road to buy the medicine while Ronnie stayed with the ailing stallion.

It was touch-and-go for an investment of $75,000—money they couldn't afford to lose.

That night, Ronnie had come to pick up a bag of sweet feed from Piney Wood Farm, hopeful that the horse would start eating if he had a different feed. Their horse farm was only four miles away. He'd left Lynn with the horse and was going to eat supper with Martha Annie, then dip up a plate to take Lynn, he had decided. Ronnie, his dark hair sprinkled with strands of gray, was almost too skinny for five feet, eleven inches because he hurried around constantly and, unless Lynn brought him lunch, he skipped that meal. But he was a lot stronger than he looked. It had been raining all day and Ronnie had been traipsing through mud, muck, and horse manure so his farm boots were covered.

He opened the screen door, pushed open the kitchen door, then remembered his boots just before stepping in. Untying them, he pushed them off.

"Hey," he said rather gloomily.

"Oh, my good heavens!" Chatty exclaimed. "What is that atrocious smell?" He pressed his hand against his chest. "I may have to depart the dinner table and hurry quickly to the powder room."

Ronnie's face turned red. Not from embarrassment but anger. His eyes narrowed and he made a fist with his right hand, then started rubbing it with his left. He was in a ripe mood for a good knockout with a fancy-dressed, refined man he had never laid eyes on.

But he could guess who he was from the stories he had heard.

"Let me set you straight. What you smell is me. I've been in the barn with a sick horse since before midnight, last night. There is none of a good mood in me. Out of courtesy to my mother-in-law, I ain't gonna kick your fancy britches back to Atlanta."

Chatty's eyes widened, and he started to shake with fear. Chatty had grown up being the target of every bully around. Of course, the disagreements were often brought on by his mouthiness. One time, when he was 10, his wisecracks resulted in five stitches above the eye.

"That'll teach you," the bigger boy said.

It didn't. Not one bit.

That night, several months earlier, Chatty was threatened with a similar fate. Stella, however, backed up by her mama, quickly stepped in.

"Ronnie, this is my friend, Chatham. He meant no harm."

Chatty nodded rapidly.

"You're the one they call 'Chatty'?"

Chatty nodded and gulped, although his delicate stomach was growing rapidly more nauseous. He had never smelled such a foulness of odor. He was fighting it. Despite his smart remark, he didn't want to jump up from the table and run somewhere to throw up. He had never had to show such ugly sickness in public before.

Ronnie had closed the door and stood angrily in place. Miss Martha Annie said, "Chatty is a wonderful person. He's a big city fella who's probably never seen the inside of a barn."

Chatty pushed back from the table, stood up, walked over and offered his hand to Ronnie. "For my remark, I apologize. There are many things about farm life with which I need to acquaint myself. May I have your forgiveness?"

Only because of Stella and how he loved her like his little sister, Ronnie shook Chatty's hand and said tersely, "Forgiven."

Chatty was now so close to the smell that he was in danger of spewing his supper all over Ronnie, which he felt, fairly certain, would make him madder. He thought quickly.

"Thank you, Ronnie. I beg your good favor for the opportunity to begin our friendship anew on a better day."

Ronnie looked at him. He had never heard anyone talk like that, but he knew what he was saying. He forced a smile. "On the condition that you pray for our sick horse to recover."

"My privilege. I shall take myself up to my room at this very moment, get down on my knees and pray. I am on *excellent* terms with the Lord." He smiled proudly. "I oversee bingo for the seniors at the Presbyterian church every Thursday night. Now, please excuse me while I go to pray." He turned on his heels and headed upstairs. Those in the kitchen could hear him running up the stairs.

"Well, I guess he's a man of his word," Ronnie commented. "Miss Martha Annie, do you have a couple of paper plates so I can dip up some supper for me and Lynn? I don't think I'll stay."

Chatty, meanwhile, was in the bathroom, cleansing himself of the supper he had just eaten. When he had stepped close to Ronnie, the smell was even more pungent, so he hurried with the apology followed by the quick scurry to the bathroom.

Then, as he had promised, he got down on his knees and prayed for the sick horse. The next afternoon, Ronnie called and asked for that city fella. Chatty took the phone from Stella.

"Buddy, I guess you are on good terms with the Lord. The stallion started perkin' up soon after I got back with our supper. Today, he is fine and dandy. Thanky, mightily."

Chatty grinned happily. "Now, any time you need me to pray, just call. I have built up quite a generous amount of goodwill equity with the Almighty."

Chatty hung up the phone and turned to Stella. "Sometimes, I just amaze myself. I'm so helpful. I'm an angel on this earth sent to help those in need."

Stella looked at him wordlessly for a moment then asked, "Does it ever become tiresome, bragging on yourself so much?"

ထ

That story flashed through Stella's mind as she prepared to introduce Chatty to Bubba. She said a silent prayer that he would watch his mouth. Bubba McCoy, was a good ol' mountain boy, but he didn't tolerate city folks well, especially those who were high and mighty. That, of course, would apply to Chatham Balsam Colquitt, IV.

Bubba had stood there, observing, and not moving one step. Chatty had not glanced Bubba's way, absorbed in Stella as he usually was. Stella took a deep breath and plunged in.

"Chatty, Bubba is a childhood friend of mine. He runs the farm." Stella held her hand out, toward Bubba. Smiling sociably, Chatty turned toward him. The smile disappeared when Chatty saw the six foot two inch, lean, handsome blonde, dressed like a cowboy he'd see on TV. Bubba had long exchanged a baseball cap years ago for a cowboy hat because it protected him from the rain and gave extra protection from the sun. He no longer had a red neck throughout the summer. In well-worn jeans and the nice barn coat with its corduroy collar turned up, Chatty spoke before he thought twice.

"Are you an actor that Stella dressed up like a 'mountain boy'?" He held up his fingers, making quotation marks. "You're too perfect-looking for the part." He turned to his best friend. "Really, Stella, you've gone over the top on this."

Bubba, so far, wasn't impressed with this friend of Stella's. "I beg your pardon, sir, but I'm a farmer and if'n you's not up to believin' me, then meet me at the cattle barn at 6 in the mornin' and you can tag along, behind me, all the day long and you'll see real quick."

That certainly didn't appeal to Chatty. He had not been dirty since he was nine years old. Bubba spoke, "Me and Stella used to help her daddy, here on the farm. My daddy was his hired help. Many are the days, we got up hay together."

"You did *what*?"

Stella stepped in to explain. "We helped our daddies to cut, bale, and load hay. I drove the truck and Bubba threw the bales in the back."

"Excuse me," said Chatty. "What did you call him?" He had been paying no attention, as usual, he was only thinking of himself.

"Bubba," Stella replied, resisting a smile as Chatty turned pale. "This is Bubba McCoy. He lives a further piece up the mountain."

Chatty fanned himself, pulled out a chair from the kitchen table and started mumbling, "I can't believe it. I just can't believe it."

"Believe what?" Stella asked, mystified. Before Chatty could answer, a knock came at the kitchen door. Martha Annie opened it to see a distinguished man dressed in a white shirt, black bow tie, and a black suit. He was carrying a large basket with several boxes stacked on top.

In a British accent, he said "Ma'am, might I have the pleasure of meeting Mrs. Jackson?"

"I'm Martha Annie Jackson. And you, I imagine, would be the beleaguered Spencer?"

"Ma'am, I am Mr. Colquitt's butler."

Bubba's eyes popped out while Chatty was still having a spell of some kind.

"A butler? In the Appalachian foothills? On Piney Wood Farm?" Bubba was shaking his head in disbelief. Then, he sorta chuckled. "I 'spect Sims Jackson never thought he'd have a fancy British butler standing in his worn out kitchen that looks the same as it did when we's kids."

"Where shall I place this silver and Wedgewood china, Mrs. Jackson?" He paused, "It's Mr. Colquitt's favorite china."

"Uh, well, uh," she looked around at her counter cluttered with mixer, toaster oven, dish rack filled with dishes that were drying, microwave, and coffee maker. "I wasn't expecting this."

"Mama, I'm sorry. I didn't know until this morning that Chatham was planning on tryin' to turn an old farmhouse into a fine manor."

Chatty was somewhat recovering from his spell. "Miss Mama, I just wanted you to have a fine Christmas."

"When did you start callin' her 'Miss Mama'?" Stella asked.

"It's better than being called Bubba!" That's when Stella knew what his spell was all about.

"You're upset that his name is Bubba?" she asked while Bubba was completely speechless by all he was seeing and hearing. Chatty had already riled him up last night.

Chatty put his hand to his forehead. "I feel faint. It never occurred to me that I would ever meet and shake hands with anyone named Bubba."

"Hey!" called out Bubba. "I don't take kindly to any such. I happen to know two other Bubbas. But ain't none of us got a fancy servant or even a fancy name. It's a hard life up here in these mountains. We work sun-up to sun-down and we still barely get by. Always worrying about how the tax bill's gonna get paid, or if our crops'll get the rain they need, or whether, all a-sudden, it'll come up a cloud with a field of hay laying, just cut. Hay that gets rained on is hay that's no good. We's just plain folks, but a finer bunch of folks you'll never find. If someone's in need, we all show up. Back in the summer, old Mr. Harkins got down with pneumonia and couldn't get his crops in. Must've been a dozen of us who put aside our work and helped that old man. The women folk, including Miss Martha Annie here, showed up and canned all that food. And we ain't got no servants to help us, neither." Chatty was nervously shifting his weight from one foot to the other and running his hands through his thick brown hair.

But Bubba wasn't finished. He moved closer until he was a foot away from Chatty. "Sir, have you ever picked green beans in hundred-degree heat with humidity stranglin' ya' half to death? This here you're lookin' at, is a common man. And, proud of it, too.

One day, when I meet up with my Maker, I kin be proud of what I done on this earth."

Bubba rubbed his hands over his face and turned to the kitchen sink where he put both hands on it and dropped his head, shaking it ever so slightly. Meanwhile, Stella gave Chatty a look that told him a lecture was coming. "Well, Mr. High and Mighty, I guess you've gotten your comeuppance." Stella had already explained what comeuppance meant.

Meekly, Chatty nodded. He walked over to the sink and put his hand on Bubba's shoulder. "Bubba," a name he never thought would slip from his lips, "please, accept my apology for my arrogance." For a moment, his mind flashed back to how he was bullied in school. He was no better than his tormentors. "I got a lot of sass in me. Sometimes, it's funny. Sometimes, not. Make that, mostly it's charming. And *sometimes*, it's unseemly. But tonight, it was the latter. May we start over? Perhaps be friends?"

Stella beamed with pride. She had never seen Chatty humble. Bubba straightened up, turned to face Chatty, and grinned. "I'd be mighty proud to be your friend." The two men shook hands. Chatty turned to Martha Annie, "Miss Mama, let's clean off this counter so Spencer can bring in all the lovely things we've brought—and let the Christmas cheer begin!"

Bubba walked over to Stella. "Sorry that had to happen."

Stella smiled and hugged his neck. "I'm proud of both of you. He's a dear. He just gets carried away."

She chuckled. "But don't worry. This humility is temporary. By tomorrow morning, he'll be back to normal."

Bubba snapped his fingers. "Speakin' of mornin'. I'll be here bright and early."

"Why so early? You don't feed the cattle until afternoon during winter. And Mama says a snowstorm is comin'."

He nodded. "S'pose to be a big one. 'Pected to start around dawn. But Ronnie and Lynn have gone to Kentucky to see his grandmother. She's hangin' on long enough to spend Christmas with them. And, well, they have a mare about to foal. She wasn't suppose to deliver for another two or three weeks only, two days back, before they left, she started showin' signs of bein' ready. Me and Ronnie loaded up her and the stallion and brought 'em on, over here, so we can keep an eye."

Stella's mind flickered over the night when she was eleven and one of their own horses delivered a solid white colt. The mama horse had no milk, so Stella raised the baby on a bottle. Sims gave the colt to Stella as a reward for her hard work. She named him Scout and he became her constant companion. He was growing old now, but still had a wonderful home on Piney Wood Farm where her mama and Bubba took good care of him.

"What time tomorrow? I'll meet you at the barn so I can see Scout."

"Probably around seven. I told the Governor I'd come by and put out hay for his bull. He's got one he rents out for breedin'."

"Doesn't he have enough money?" Stella asked with a loving smile. McCager Burnett might have been raised a poor mountain boy, but now he was a very rich Atlanta lawyer, though mostly retired, and a former congressman and governor.

Bubba smiled fondly. "He does it more to help the folks around here. He barely charges. Just enough so they can keep their pride. He's still got him a real heart for us mountain folks. Anyway, I look after things when they're elsewhere. He likes to piddle on the farm when he's here, but, with the storm comin', I don't want him out in the weather." Bubba looked over her fancy clothes. "You bring you any farmin' clothes?"

She grinned. "You can bet your last dime, I did."

He patted her on the shoulder. "Then I'll see you in the barn come mornin'."

He went over to say goodbye to the rest where Miss Martha Annie and Spencer were being directed by Chatty, who had quickly regained his glory. Yet, everyone was in high spirits and friendly. Bubba had just closed the door when Stella thought of something. She ran out, calling for Bubba who was opening the door of his truck.

"Hey, Bubs, by any chance, do I have *you* to thank for decorating our old hay truck?"

He grinned. "I did the lights and generator. Lynn got an artist-friend to letter the signs." He winked. "Merry Christmas."

With that, he jumped in the truck while she stood there, shivering in the cold, watching his red taillights disappear down the gravel road.

Chapter Five

Alva Burnett had been up long before a glimpse of dawn. She was helping Martha Annie with Christmas Day lunch. As is the way of Southerners, particularly those from the mountains, they were cooking up way too much food, but both women enjoyed cooking, especially during the holidays.

Alva had just slid three cake pans into the oven when her husband, McCager Burnett, came into the kitchen, yawning. She smiled. "It looks like you could use a cup of coffee."

"If you please, Miss Alva." Rubbing his neck, he sat down at the old, battered kitchen table that Alva's granddaddy had built for his daughter, Irene, when Alva's parents married. Alva's daddy had built this little farmhouse mostly with help from his wife, but their family pitched in whenever they had time. In the end, it turned into a fine-looking house with a kitchen large enough to eat in and a table big enough to spread a gardenful of vegetables so Miss Irene and Alva could work them and put them up to have for eating in the winter months. Under the house was a root cellar formed partially from the cold red clay with a couple windows. It could be entered by a staircase from the top or a back door. There, they stored all the vegetables they had "put up" from the summer garden as well as potatoes, carrots, jams, and jellies. Memories of her simple but enormously happy childhood were a daily part of Miss Alva's memories. Sometimes, she thought of her mama, picturing her coming back in the morning, holding her apron up, filled with fresh eggs. After breakfast, she went to milk the cow and bring back a bucket of warm milk.

When Alva wasn't in school, she sat on a small stool beside a pottery churn, with milk in it, using both hands, plunging it up and down for what seemed like an endless amount of time. When Alva had finished, her mama separated it into buttermilk. Then, Alva would churn a bit longer to make butter. There, in the shadow of Blood Mountain, where the Appalachian Trail begins and where two warring tribes battled so furiously, for days, that blood ran down in massive streams, no one would have guessed that little Alva Murphy would grow up to become the wife of such an important man. McCager Burnett, who grew up some fifty or so miles away in Turniptown, was first a U.S. congressman for two terms and then had come back to Georgia to serve as governor for two terms. Now, the Burnetts split their time between a beautiful house in Atlanta's Buckhead and an even prettier one on Sea Island, off the coast of Georgia, while McCager still had a hand in the legal practice where he was senior partner.

But this little farmhouse, with a front porch poured from concrete, with strong pillars that were brick halfway up then wood, was their favorite place to be. On the drive up, as each was silently enjoying the countryside and returning to the roots of their raising, McCager had said, "Do you realize, Miss Alva, that we're nothing but old mountain folks who came down from the hills and got lucky? Sure, we've worked hard. We set about serving our fellow man and always God Almighty. Yet, we're mighty blessed." Alva's brother had died before their mother had, so when he passed away, she left the farm to Alva.

She nodded her head, now mostly silver. "I shouldn't complain and my daddy taught me to never, under any condition, question God. But life would be overflowing if we had been blessed with children."

Cager, as he was called except when he was respected with the title of governor nodded quietly. The first time he laid eyes on Alva Murphy at North Georgia College, his heart had been hers. Now, it had belonged to her for almost fifty years, so he couldn't imagine sharing it with anyone else. Yes, he could have embraced children happily at one time, but now they had about as perfect a life as anyone could enjoy.

She sighed sweetly. "But we do have dear Chatham."

McCager shook his head and said gruffly but humorously, "Yes, we do. Just like the Apostle Paul who could never rid himself of that thorn in his side."

"McCager!" she chastised teasingly and they laughed. The Governor was the only one who could keep Chatty straight. He toed the line when he was around the Governor and kept a hold, somewhat, on his tongue.

They were planning to spend three weeks up here, and this was their fourth morning since their arrival. "Did you sleep well last night, my dear?" she asked as she poured him a cup of coffee.

"I sleep like a baby when I'm here in these mountains. That's why I'm still yawning!"

"How about eggs, bacon, and toast?" she asked. "I would fix a pan of biscuits but I just put a cake in the oven. Since snow is expected, Martha Annie and I decided we should skip the late breakfast and get ready for tomorrow."

He perked up. "One of those fine, caramel cakes?"

She nodded. "It's Chatty's favorite."

"And your husband's, if that matters any."

She laughed. "It matters most! Oh, McCager, look out the kitchen window. It's spitting snow."

He turned in his chair. "Yes, ma'am, it is. They say a storm is comin'. Can't remember snow at Christmas in quite a while."

"My Uncle Oscar told me that it used to snow several inches every Christmas when he was a boy."

"Climate change," he snickered. McCager Burnett was one politician who didn't believe in any such. He put his arm around his wife and watched the small flakes swirling around in the air.

"What time will Pepper be here?" the Governor asked as he caught a glimpse of Bubba getting into his truck.

"Around ten."

A delicious, devilish thought crept into his mind. "Has Chatty met Bubba yet?"

"I don't know."

"Miss Alva, I think I'll skip breakfast this morning." She turned around and looked at him, surprised. "I think I'll go over to Sims Jackson's farm and take in a little entertainment." He winked, grabbed his jacket off the coat hook, and headed out the door, chuckling to himself.

ca

Stella sat down in her grandmother's rocking chair to pull on her socks and boots. It would be cold in the barn, so she had on thin but warm silk underwear, flannel-lined jeans, and a thick sweater. With all that and her barn coat and a hat, she ought to be warm enough. As she was tying up her last boot, she glanced through the lace curtains. Then, reaching over, she pulled them back.

"Well, I'll be dogged. It *is* snowing on Christmas Eve!"

As a special surprise, her mama had decorated the Christmas tree with tinsel—just as she and Lynn had done when they were growing up. She almost cried when she saw it, while Chatty stared for a moment then exclaimed, "*What* is that? Did you cut up a box of aluminum foil?"

Stella made a face at him. "When we were growing up, we'd go out and find a tree. Bubba would bring it back for us then Lynn and I decorated. We put tinsel like this on it. It's a fine art."

"I'm sure it is," Chatty replied, sarcastically.

"No, truly. It tangles easily so you have to be patient when taking it out of the box. Then, it has to be placed, appropriately, so that it looks like a tumbling waterfall."

"When I was a child, my mother hired professional decorators to come in and design our entire house for Christmas. Differently, every year." Chatham tossed his head arrogantly.

"I'm sure that was very rewarding and provided you with a lifetime of memories," Stella replied, still admiring the tree.

Chatty spread his hands. "As just proven. May I also mention that our housekeeper made delicious hot chocolate for me to enjoy as I oversaw the operation?"

Stella turned to him. "You oversaw the operation? How old were you?"

"I began at the age of four."

Stella thought back on that conversation from the previous night as she watched the snow blowing around. Tinsel and snow. A real Appalachian Christmas.

"No amount of money could buy this from me. No amount." Her thoughts turned serious, and it began occurring to her that the mountains were born in her. She tried to be a fancy socialite and flopped miserably—and publicly, at that. She had loved, greatly, the months she'd recently been living on St. Simons Island but now she could feel that no place but these mountains would ever be home to her. The Governor had said this to her a couple of times, always reminding her, "Stella, there's nothing wrong with enjoying the finer things in life. Just don't ever forget where you came from and what Sims Jackson would expect of you."

"Oh, dear Daddy." She whispered at the memory. She picked up her coat, a wool brimmed hat, and skipped down the squeaky steps. Hearing conversation in the kitchen, Stella walked in to find her mama and Chatty talking and laughing, happily.

"What are you doin' up so early?" she asked, suspiciously. Typically, Chatham Balsam Colquitt IV never turned over in bed before 9:30 or 10 o'clock.

"Oh, Stella," Chatty replied, dropping his chin in his hand. "I have spent an entire night in pure agony. That bed is too small for me."

"Or could you be too big for the bed?"

He shot her a look of irritation. "Stella Faye Jackson Bankwell, sometimes you can be just mean, mean, mean."

"As though you weren't mean about the tinsel on the Christmas tree." She raised an eyebrow and waited for his response.

"Well, precious Stella, you have to admit that it's a little low class. Not as bad as that scene you made at the country club with Annabelle Honeycutt. But close." He held up his finger and thumb almost touching. She glared at him as she put on her barn coat.

"Now, listen, children, I'm not gonna have y'all fussin' in this house. Not now. Not when we're celebrating the birth of the baby Jesus. It's Christmas and snow's comin'."

"Miss Mama, I will be very good. I promise." He leaned toward her and whispered, "but Stella started it. Yes, she did, Miss Mama."

Stella opened her mouth to reply when she suddenly felt movement behind her. She turned to see Spencer passing by with a silver tray on which there was a silver coffee service, two fine china cups, and saucer. Elegantly, he served them, then made a slight bow to Stella.

"Ms. Bankwell, shall I secure a cup for you?"

Stella walked over to her mama's battered cupboard and pulled out two tall, plastic coffee mugs. "Spencer, will you fill these, please, and add cream? I'd be much obliged."

"Thank you," she said when he finished. She adjusted the hat on her head. "Mama, I expect the storm to be here shortly. I saw it spitting snow from my window."

Chatty nearly choked on his coffee. "Spitting snow! What in the heavens does 'spitting snow' mean?"

Stella and her Mama looked at each other, puzzled.

"You've never heard that sayin'?" Martha Annie asked.

"Never in the least-finest moment of my life." Before anyone could reply, there was a tap on the kitchen door and the Governor stuck his head inside. "Mind if I come in?"

Martha Annie stood up and walked over to hug their family friend and welcome him home for Christmas. After a round of good mornings, McCager Burnett, mountain man that he was, looked over to see Spencer placing items on a fancy silver tray in front of a red pottery rooster with a few chips here and there. Cager stood there, shaking his head.

"Chatham, there will never be another like you. Probably, hasn't ever been."

Chatham smiled charmingly. "Governor, it was my desire to give Miss Mama an unforgettable Christmas."

"Miss Mama?" Chatham had, indeed, surprised the Governor again. Meanwhile, Stella was pulling on her gloves.

"If you find out where that 'Miss Mama' business came from, let me know," Stella said over her back as Spencer opened the door to let her out with the cups of coffee.

The Governor turned to Martha Annie, "Miss Mama, it was spitting snow when I left the house but it's beginning to snow, full-on."

Exasperated, Chatty almost yelled. "Will someone please tell me what 'spitting snow' means?"

The Governor, hanging his coat over the back of the chair, responded, "It's Appalachian talk." He paused a moment. "But, come to think of it, someone with a butler would never understand."

Chatham shrugged nonchalantly and took a sip of coffee. He'd rather have a butler than understand Appalachian language, anyway.

Chapter Six

It wasn't that US Marshal Jackson Culpepper was indispensable. It was that he was dependable and smart, which is why the head of the Atlanta office had asked if there was any way that he could work on Christmas Eve.

Pepper was firm with his "no." Normally, whenever the US Marshal Service needed him, Pepper was there to do it. That was why, when he requested that his six-month assignment to Glynco as an instructor be extended indefinitely, they had agreed with the stipulation that if he was needed to work a case, he would oblige. There was only one reason that he wanted to remain in Glynn County, Georgia, and that was the beautiful Stella Bankwell. He had been married to his work and, along the way, the handsome Marshal had broken plenty of hearts. Stella had such an effect on him that he was shy, romantically. They had shared many dinners on St. Simons, and an occasional movie, but he was yet to hold her hand or kiss her. To him, she felt aloof, so he kept a certain distance. Pride. That's what held him back. He was highly touted in the Marshal Service for his bravery and with the other women, he always had the upper hand with his charm and good looks.

Not this time. Stella held all the cards. So, normally, he would have agreed to work over Christmas. But he was not going to miss two days in the mountains with Stella. Too, he had never seen the lower Appalachians. Stella talked endlessly of the fabulous hardwood trees and pines that covered the mountains, the rivers, the pastureland that stretched forever, and the waterfall near her home.

He glanced at the clock. One more hour and he should be there. Miss Alva had warned him that there was very little cell service in the hollow where they lived so she had given him the number to their landline. He called Miss Alva to tell her where he was and she asked, as he would've expected, should she have a late breakfast ready or did he want to wait for lunch? "We are not having a late breakfast with the Jacksons because of the bad weather coming. We hope to get Christmas lunch fixed."

She chuckled. "As a matter of fact, you can have McCager's breakfast. He sat down to eat then skipped out and hurried over to Sims' farm." She chuckled again. "A wonderful young man named Bubba McCoy runs the farm for Martha Annie and helps us around here, too. His daddy, Rooster, was Sims' right hand. He still helps during hay season and whenever Bubba needs him. Bubba is an Appalachians boy through and through. So, when Cager discovered that Chatty was about to meet up with Bubba, he jumped up from the table and headed out the door saying he wasn't going to miss the entertainment. Chatty has never seen the likes of Bubba and vice versa. It'll make for a grand Christmas."

Pepper tried to picture in his mind the meeting of the debonair, well-polished Chatty to a roughed mountain boy. And, as he did, he had to admit it would be very amusing.

"I'll come straight to your farm, then maybe we can go over to Stella's where I can see that for myself. I should be there in about an hour."

Miss Alva hung up the phone and started toward the bedroom to make the bed when there was a knock at the kitchen door. She peeped around the curtain and saw that it was their neighbor, Daniel Madison. He and his wife, Melissa, had bought the fifteen acres, two years ago, that Miss Alva's daddy had sold when her mother was sick. The Madisons had purchased it two years ago from the original buyers. They were a lovely young couple and the Burnetts thought the world of them. Daniel worked for the Forestry Service and farmed a bit on the side. They were both hard workers. Melissa didn't hesitate to help Daniel outside. It was a familiar sight to see her riding the lawn mower or tractor, cutting the yard and pastures. They had been married for fifteen years and had prayed diligently for a baby. Now, their prayers were about to be answered. Melissa was heavy with child, nearing her due date.

"Daniel, what a lovely surprise. Come in, out of the cold. That snowfall is getting heavier. Looks like it's getting close to two inches."

Daniel stomped the snow off his feet before entering and said, "Yes, Mrs. Burnett, I'd say you're right."

In his hands, he held a container. "Melissa wanted me to bring this over to y'all. Christmas cookies. The best you'll ever taste."

"Oh, my goodness, thank you! McCager loves nothing better than a good cookie."

"That's her grandmother's recipe. They're kinda like the teacakes my grandmother used to make but hers was thicker."

"Come in and sit a spell." She motioned toward the living room. Miss Alva couldn't help it. When she came home to her mountains, she fell into Appalachian speech.

"Well, just for a few minutes. I don't want to leave Melissa alone for too long." She was still two weeks away from her due date, but he wasn't taking any chances if he could avoid it. He had been treating her like a precious piece of china. He insisted that she eat well and get a lot of rest.

"How's Melissa feelin'?" Miss Alva inquired.

"She's pretty uncomfortable—whether she's sittin' or layin'. That's why we have three dozen Christmas cookies. She's more comfortable standin'. Before I come over here, I made her lay down."

"It won't be long now, y'all won't be getting any sleep." She smiled, thinking again that she wished she'd had that opportunity.

"I can't wait. We thank the good Lord every day." He stood up. "I best be goin'. I'm gonna make her some vegetable soup for lunch."

Miss Alva walked Daniel to the door. "It's gonna be a very Merry Christmas around here. We can all count our blessings."

"Yes, ma'am, we shore can." Daniel tipped his hat as he opened the door. "You and the Governor call me to see if I kin help you. If this snow keeps up, we're liable to lose power. Y'all got plenty of firewood, just in case?"

She smiled and patted him on the shoulder. "We're good. Y'all call us if *we* can help."

"Yes, ma'am. Merry Christmas." With that, he was gone, and Miss Alva whispered a little prayer to thank the Lord for blessing the Madisons.

ꕤ

The Governor was plenty disappointed to learn that he had missed out on Chatty meeting Bubba. He joined Martha Annie and Chatty at the kitchen table while Spencer stood by, ready to attend to anything they needed. Chatty carried on and on about "tshis creature named Bubba" while Spencer poured coffee for the table.

"Did it ever occur to you to give Spencer some time off during Christmas rather than dragging him up to the mountains?" the Governor asked.

"No," Chatty said simply as he took another sip of coffee.

Aggravated, the Governor shook his head. "Never have I ever seen the likes of you." Just as Miss Alva did, Cager took to falling back into Appalachian language whenever he returned to the mountains.

"Thank you, Governor, for the compliment."

"It wasn't a compliment," he replied gruffly. "Miss Martha Annie and Miss Alva are plenty capable of taking care of us for Christmas."

"But they wouldn't have had silver serving pieces which are over a century old. And this beautiful china that I flew all the way to London to select, personally. Governor, I'm a great deal more considerate than you credit me. I was thinking solely of Miss Mama and Miss Alva."

"Miss Mama?" The Governor asked quizzically.

"Yes, Miss Mama." Chatty motioned toward Martha Annie.

The Governor simply shook his head.

"Cager, I wish you had been here to see the look on Chatty's face when he saw Bubba." she laughed gaily. She had one of the prettiest laughs anyone had ever heard. "It was priceless."

"Has he met Rooster yet?"

Chatty's eyes flew open, wide. "What's a Rooster?"

ଓ

When Stella had gotten to the barn a couple of hours earlier, she found that Bubba was already there, tending to Fancy Sadie, the expectant mare.

"How's she doing?" Stella asked.

"Pretty ripe for deliverin'."

The barn had four stalls. The father stallion was in the stall next to Fancy Sadie. Between each stall was a window where the stallion stuck his head through, from time to time, to check on things—as when he first heard Stella's voice. She giggled. The simple pleasures of mountain life brought such joy to Stella. Here she was, back in the place that meant the most to her, along with her Mama and Bubba, her childhood friend.

"What's his name?" she asked Bubba, admiring the beautiful black stallion with a shining coat. She could understand why Lynn and Ronnie had spent $75,000 on him. In the two years since they bought him, they had almost made their money back in stud fees. According to them, this stallion produced excellent offspring, and other breeders were more than willing to pay the stud fees for a loan out.

"I don't rightly know. He's got some high falutin' registered name, but Lynn and Ronnie just call him 'Big Black.'"

"He's a beauty, for sure." She walked over to the third stall as joy swept over her and she clapped her hands like child. "There's my precious Scout," she said of the horse she had adored since she was eleven. He threw back his head and neighed, just as happy to see her. Bubba walked over to enjoy the reunion. He thought about how Stella had only grown more beautiful with time. As she hugged Scout and kissed his velvety nose, her red hair shone stunningly. Turning to Bubba, Stella felt her heart stir. After all these years, she still had a crush on him. In that instance, Stella wondered why she had ever left this farm and these mountains.

It was her true home.

Chapter Seven

As the US Marshal, Jackson Culpepper, drove the last twenty miles to the Burnetts' farm, he began to understand why Stella had bragged, repeatedly, on the beauty of the Appalachian Mountains.

He crossed a bridge over a lazy river that rippled over polished rock, then past the side of a mountain from which sprang a tiny spring of water that dribbled over the rock, puddling by the side of a highway. Farmland was vast, much of it covered with grazing cattle. It seemed there was a church every two miles. Up on a hill was a Methodist church called Mt. Pleasant, its snow-covered steeple standing picturesque and overlooking the valley below. He traveled another mile and saw a Baptist church, Antioch, on the right with a snow-covered dirt road leading up to a simple, white clapboard sanctuary. Both churches were surrounded by cemeteries, facing to the east. It occurred to Pepper that he had never seen churches with graveyards. In Memphis, where he grew up, and in Glynn County, churches mostly set by themselves and the cemeteries were off somewhere on separate land, usually surrounded by fences and a couple of gates. All denominations were buried together. He chuckled a bit at the thought that the Baptists and Methodists weren't buried together.

Just as he finished the small laugh, the lower mountain land seemed to rise up majestically and wrapped its welcoming arms around him. The road wound gently through beautiful maples and oaks that towered on each side. In the snow that was piling up steadily, the bare trees stood out like lovely gems. Even with the windows up, he could feel the stillness that spread under the shade of the great Appalachians and the snow, of course, which made it even quieter. As he approached their driveway, guided by GPS, he was stunned to see the great mountain that stood less than a mile away. He turned onto the drive to find the sweet farmhouse and the stream that ran beside it. In that moment, he knew completely why Stella always felt drawn to her mountain home. It looked and felt like a dream. Grateful for his four-wheel-drive SUV, issued to him by the US Marshals Service, he climbed the drive. After stepping out of the car, he took a moment to absorb the natural beauty. Across the road lay an expansive field. That, he reasoned, was Stella's family farm. He had passed a drive half a mile earlier.

"You made it!" called out Miss Alva. "Come on in and let me feed you. Then, we'll go over to the Jacksons." She winked as he reached to hug her. "I feel certain that's what brought you here. Stella."

ꕤ

At the kitchen table, Martha Annie had told the Governor all about the horse, ready to foal, and how Lynn and Ronnie had no choice but to keep with their plans to go to Kentucky since his grandmother was pushing away death until she could see them again.

Cager slapped his hand on the table. "Now, this is exciting! This is what farm life's all about—new life springing forth, whether its livestock or crops. Let's go out to barn right now."

He looked over at Chatty, who was expensively attired in custom made slacks, a shirt, and a red cashmere sweater. He peeped under the table to ascertain that Chatty was also wearing custom-made loafers.

"Chatty, have you ever seen a barn?" he asked, with a twinkle in his eye.

"Yes, sir. From the outside."

"Let me rephrase. Have you ever seen the *inside* of a barn?"

"Of course not. Governor, that's a silly question. You've seen my mansions. We don't even have a barn on the plantation property. I think there was one, a long time ago, but it burned down."

"Them all the clothes you got? Because you're going to the barn. I mean to see to that, and I don't think you want to walk in the snow in those fancy shoes."

"I have a heavy, more casual overcoat but I don't have any other shoes that were not crafted especially for me." As was normal, he said it in a haughty way.

McCager Burnett rolled his eyes. He and Chatty's Miss Mama looked at each other. Spencer was busy preparing a lunch of soup and salad. He had roasted a chicken to use in his personal recipe. Finally, Martha Annie, always one to think of a solution, asked Chatty, "What size shoe do you wear?"

"Eleven."

She nodded and smiled. "Sims wore an eleven and a half. I still have a pair of his farm boots upstairs. You can wear them, and if they're too large you'll put on an extra pair of socks."

The expressions on Chatty's face went from shock to horror to downright fear. And McCager Burnett enjoyed every moment.

"Chatty, what's the problem?"

The normally well-spoken, self-assured, often over-confident Chatham Balsam Colquitt IV rubbed his chin. Cager noticed the slight tremble in his hand. When he answered, he stuttered.

"Uh, well it, uh, it's just that..." He stopped. "Miss Mama, don't take this wrong or disrespectful but I've never worn hand-me-downs. It's rather upsetting to my constitution."

With his back to the table, Chatty couldn't see the grin on his British-raised butler but he could witness the joyful laughter of the Governor and Miss Mama.

"Merry Christmas, Chatty," the Governor boomed. "We have presented you with the gorgeous mountains in the snow and now you will receive, as our special gift to you, a new experience."

Spencer brought a large silver tray to the table and set an antique, porcelain tureen filled with steaming hot soup at the center.

"May I have the privilege of serving you, Ma'am," he asked Miss Mama. She smiled and said, "Why, yes, please."

To Chatty, she said, "I could git used to this real fast." While Spencer ladled the soup into the Wedgewood china bowl, she promised, "As soon as we finish lunch, I'll get Sims' boots."

Chatty looked terrified and mumbled, "I think I've lost my appetite."

ꝏ

Bubba scratched his head. He was standing in the fourth stall of the barn, scooping up sweet feed for Fancy Sadie, Big Black, and Scout. He pondered for a long while until Stella, who was still loving on Scout, asked, "What's the matter?"

"I don't know. It's the strangest thing but this feed is goin' down faster than I'm usin' it."

She shrugged. "Probably raccoons."

"Naw, ain't that. Old Man Rance Cain 'coon hunts all the time. Ain't nary a one can escape that rascal."

"Possums?"

"They don't take a likin' to sweet feed. This has been goin' on for weeks now."

After the feedings, Stella and Bubba sat down on a bales of hay. For a long time, neither spoke until Bubba removed his hat and ran his hands through his hair. He looked around the barn as if seeing it for the first time—the saddles, bridles, buckets, mule harness, stacks of hay and feed.

"Lotta memories in this ol' barn," Bubba said, sounding sad.

Stella nodded and slipped her arm through his. She scooted closer to him. Feelings of warmth, love, and nostalgia came over her. Bubba knew her like no one else ever could. He knew her daddy—and Sims Jackson loved him like the son he never had. She could remember Bubba making every step that Sims made. He loved him as much as he loved his own daddy, Rooster.

"If only we knew then what we know now about life," she said, wistful.

Suddenly, the barn door swung open, and the snow blew in. It was now five inches deep. McCager Burnett strode inside, in all his authority, with a timid Chatty following behind. He had changed into custom-made khakis which Miss Mama had stuffed inside Sims' boots so they wouldn't get wet in the snow. He wore a heavy, knee-length coat and a red knit sock cap. It was one of the most ridiculous sights Stella had ever seen, and she threw back her head, laughing.

"Is that Chatham Balsam Colquitt IV, scion of Atlanta's most elite? In farm boots and a sock cap?"

Chatty tossed Stella an annoyed look but then was suddenly captivated by what he saw. With the wonderment of a child, he looked around the barn, studying it, then moved slowly toward Fancy Sadie.

"This is what the inside of a barn looks like?" he asked, speaking softly. Fancy Sadie stuck her head through the stall door and neighed. She took an immediate liking to Chatty and nuzzled his hand, which led him to gently stroke her face. "This is magical."

Cager and Stella looked at each other, stunned by what they were witnessing. She and Bubba stood up as he raised his hat, ran his fingers through his hair, then replaced his hat back on his head and walked over to Chatty and Fancy Sadie.

"This here is the mare 'bout to foal. Name's Fancy Sadie."

Puzzled, Chatty asked, "What does that mean?"

"She's gonna have a baby. Any time."

"How marvelous!" Which, most likely, was the first time that word had ever been used in that barn. An idea struck Chatty, and he clapped his hands together, exclaiming merrily, "The decorations I brought from Atlanta! I'll decorate the stall and make it cheery for our Christmas baby." Before anyone could speak—they had all been rendered speechless—the oddly-dressed Chatty dashed out of the barn, racing happily through the snow, toward the waiting Christmas decorations in his SUV.

ଓଃ

Daniel hadn't said anything, but he noticed that Melissa was squirming, uncomfortably, in her rocker as well as getting up and down a lot. She'd walk the room a bit then sit back down.

Outside, the snow continued to fall and stacked up to eight inches by three p.m. Daniel looked out the window. It showed no sign of letting up. He went out to the carport and got two flashlights, then found some candles and matches. He stacked more firewood next to the wood burning potbelly stove. And as he threw another log into the fire, Melissa said, "Honey, I think I'll lay down awhile."

Worry tugged at Daniel. "Missy, are you okay?"

"I don't know. I think so."

"Think so?"

She nodded and headed toward the bedroom just as the lights flickered.

Chapter Eight

Back at the house, Martha Annie, or Miss Mama as Chatty had taken to calling her, was taking command of the kitchen—including Chatty's butler, Spencer.

"Now, Spencer, we's 'bout to face a little crisis here. Not nothin' we ain't able to handle but we gotta git on it."

"Yes, Madam. May I inquire as to what this crisis might entail?"

She looked at Spencer and smiled. She suspected he had never been in a house without electricity. But, in those mountains, where utilities were spare to begin with, this kind of snow would, according to the TV weatherman, turn into a blizzard. There would be no way to avoid the loss of power if it stacked up to a foot or more. When the temperature started dropping at nightfall, the snow covering the power lines would freeze and break. During these times, Martha Annie never failed to pray for the linemen who'd be called out by Amicalola EMC, to leave their families, the warmth of their homes, to endanger their lives by trying to restore power.

"It's the snow storm. Up here in these mountains, we always lose power if there's enough snow or ice.

Sommers 'round five years ago, we were without electricity for almost a week. I sat by the fireplace to stay warm and did my sleepin' on the couch. It was so cold in here that all my house plants died." She nodded. "Shore did."

Spencer, who had been properly trained not to show emotion of any kind while on duty or never to tell anything he saw in the house of his master, could not hold back the slight surprise and panic in the pupils of his eyes, though his face moved not a muscle. His training at the British Butler Institute had repeatedly stressed that a proper butler is always prepared for the unexpected, regardless of the circumstances. However, the British Butler Institute had most likely never turned out a graduate who faced an Appalachian snowstorm that threatened to take out the electricity.

"Madam, I shall rise to the occasion." Spencer offered a small bow, placing his arm across his mid-section. He even smiled ever-so-slightly. "How may I assist in this time of trouble which appears to be arriving?"

Martha Annie gave him a broad smile. "Spencer, I knew I could count on you." For some time now, she had been thawing a large turkey in the refrigerator. Fortunately, it was completely thawed and ready to cook. She reached over and set the oven.

"Spencer, in times like these, it calls for old-fashioned ingenuity. I'm gonna set this oven to 500 degrees and get it real hot. As you may know, a turkey should begin cooking on 350 degrees."

"No Madam, I was not aware of that. Mr. Colquitt has a full-time chef. I am only effective at simple cooking such as preparing chicken salad, trays to serve with cocktails, and the occasional peanut butter and jelly sandwich when Mr. Colquitt requests it."

She couldn't help it. She had to laugh at the thought of the high society Chatham eating a peanut butter and jelly sandwich. Spencer tilted his head, the closest he would come to expression.

"Now, Spencer, in these mountains, we don't 'teach'. We 'learn' you."

"Yes, Madam. I am a lifelong admirer of Mr. Shakespeare. In the short time, I have had the pleasure of being here, I have heard many Shakespearean words and phrases. I also took notice of hearing scriptures from the King James Bible. In England, it's owned by The Crown, you may know, and read exclusively in the Church of England. Our wonderful Queen Elizabeth, now sadly departed to her home in glory, was a dedicated reader of the King James Bible. He, King James, of course, being part of her bloodline."

This was, perhaps, the most words that Spencer had uttered since he had come into Chatty's employ fifteen years earlier—except when he called back to Cotswolds, his home, or spoke to Ruby, the chef. As for Martha Annie, oddly enough, she felt she had found a kindred spirit in a man who came from a land she had never seen. She'd not even been on a plane though Stella, when she was married to Asher Bankwell, had pleaded with her many times to fly with her to New York City, Dallas, or someplace different from the mountains.

"No, Stella, the good Lord put me here in these mountains. This is where the Almighty wants me, and this is where I aim to stay."

To Spencer, she said, "You fit better in these mountains than you figure. The King James Bible is the only one used in these parts. We're a-stickin' to it, too. Well, let's get busy. It's hard to tell how long the electricity will last. We'll put the turkey in at 500 degrees and git it started real good. Then, we'll turn it down to 400. If'n the power goes, we'll duct tape the oven door tight, to trap the heat. Hopefully, that'll finish cookin' it. I have the dressin' ready in the fridge, so I'll put that in and bake it, too. It should only take forty minutes."

"Yes, Madam." He paused. "Might I inquire as to what is 'duct tape'? Additionally, I have never heard the term 'dressing' as applied to cooking."

"Duct tape, I'll show ya later. Dressin' is similar to what you call stuffin'. 'Cept we don't put it in the turkey. My mama was known for her dressin' so I make it like she did. Before y'all got here, I cooked a small chicken and cornbread. I tore the chicken into pieces, mixed it with cornbread, and the broth of the chicken." She was pulling a very large pan out of the refrigerator as she spoke. She showed it to Spencer, who nodded, then slid it into the oven. Next, she got a much bigger pan, took the turkey out, placed it in the pan, and put that in the oven. Just as she finished, the telephone rang.

"Hey, Alva. I just put the turkey and dressin' in the oven. Surely, we'll lose power. It's snowin' harder. On top of that, we've got a horse in the barn about to foal. Cager's out there, joinin' the fun. Do you think it'd be a good idea to start your casseroles cookin'?" She listened for a bit.

"Good. That's good. And you say that Pepper's over there?" A moment. "Oh, I knowed he was comin'. Stella done told me. I'm glad he made it before the roads got bad. Okay, y'all come over soon as you can. Good to know that Pepper has a four-wheel drive vee-hicle." A mountain pronunciation. They, too, said "si-reen" rather than "siren".

She placed the receiver back on the hook. It was a pink wall phone that had been hanging there for twenty-five years. She was always amazed that her daughters were buying cellular phones every two or three years. This phone had cost eight dollars, paid over time to the Standard Phone Company, and lasted all these years. The last cell phone that Lynn bought cost six hundred dollars for use in a place where there was very little service.

Lynn said, "Well, just in case it works when I need it. Too, we pull a trailer with horses a good bit of the time so you never know when it might work at the right time."

"Madam, in what way may I now assist you?" Spencer, too, had found a kindred spirit.

Before she could answer, the kitchen door opened and the comical figure of Chatty, with his pants still stuck inside Sims' boots, and the red sock cap that she had knitted years ago, practically danced into the kitchen. A joy that seemed to glow covered his entire body. He was singing *Jingle Bells*.

"Spencer, come with me. We have to get the Christmas decorations from the car. We're expecting a new baby on Piney Wood Farm, and we need to festively decorate the stall and barn. A Christmas baby shall arrive soon. Miss Mama, this is a happy day!"

Miss Mama stepped between Chatty and Spencer. Chatty was about to see a side of Martha Annie Jackson he had never glimpsed.

"Chatham, Spencer is stayin' right here with me." She gave him a no-nonsense look which took him aback. "We're 'spectin' the electricity to go out anytime. We're tryin' to get food ready. We're also going to fill two ice chests with snow to keep the milk and other perishables cold. Besides, look at him." She motioned to Spencer who was wearing his bow tie and normal, formal attire, including black patent leather, lace up shoes. Chatty looked at him and Miss Mama, who noted his bewilderment.

"Oh, Chatty, are you *that* citified? We rustled up barn clothes for you as best we could. If I could spare him, we couldn't find clothes and shoes to fit him to drag through the snow. He's gonna make sandwiches while I make sweet tea. If we don't finish before the power goes out, we'll have no food."

This little bit of information got Chatty's attention immediately. His head snapped back, and his eyes widened. "No food?! Nothing to eat?!" he squawked. "Why, that would be downright tragic."

"Yeah," she replied. "And it could happen. No food. No lights. No heat except for the fireplace."

Chatty was thunderstruck, trying to absorb all he was hearing. Finally, he sighed heavily. "Stella never told me that I might be exposed to such primitive conditions."

"Mr. Colquitt, you're 'bout to see a whole different side of life than you've ever known." A sly smile touched Martha Annie's lips. "And, I got a feelin', it'll do you a world of good."

Chatty dropped his head but out of the corner of his eye, he saw four strange looking glass items, about twelve inches high, on the kitchen table. He turned to look at them, studying on them for several seconds.

"Miss Mama, what on earth are those? Some kind of antiques?"

Before she spoke, the thought crossed her mind that this was the beginning of a much-needed education for Chatham Balsam Colquitt, IV. She walked to the table.

"These are kerosene lanterns," she explained. She pulled a globe off and pointed to a wide, white cord inside. "This is the wick. See here, it touches the bottom of the globe? That there is kerosene, and the wick draws it from the bottom. These belonged to my grandparents. They've come to great use over the years.

When the lights go out, we will have light with these." She put her fingers on the sturdy knob. "You adjust how much light you get with this." She turned the knob and the wick rose. "The higher the wick, the more light there you get."

"You mean when the lights go, we'll use these to illuminate?"

She nodded. "Until President Franklin D. Roosevelt discovered the plight of the mountain and rural folks who had no electricity, my parents growed up with their mama's cookin' on stoves that used firewood, and read the Bible, the King James version"—she turned and winked at Spencer—"right beside the fireplace with one of the lamps glowin' on a nearby table. Thanks to President Roosevelt comin' down to Georgia often to the Little White House, he saw our needs. And there were plenty. He moved right quick to establish the Electric Membership Cooperations that would build power lines. World War II was almost over before it got to these mountains. I remember as a little girl that they strung one light down on a cord over the kitchen table. Just a light bulb. On the day they hooked up my grandmama's electricity, we sat around the table, waitin' to see the light. I'll never forget that."

It was all too much for Chatty to handle. He felt like he was in a Third World country and that he had spent his life avoiding any such places. He nodded. "I'm sorry, Miss Mama, you had such a hard time."

"I'm not complainin'," she responded. "It made me a better person. I have more sympathy for those who suffer."

Chatty, astounded by this revelation, could only think of one thing to say. "When I was in the ninth grade, I prepared an essay on President Roosevelt." Pause. Then a slight frown. "I got a C-."

Miss Mama placed her hand over her mouth to hide the smile that was trying to take form. "Well, maybe now that you know this, you could get an A."

All a-sudden, Chatty's cheery mood returned. He clapped his hands together. "Since I must handle all the Christmas decorations in the stall, I have to hurry. Fancy Sadie could deliver any time now."

Spencer handed him the car keys. "Sir, you will need these. I suggest pressing this button. It will open where the decorations are stored, in back."

"Thank you, Spencer." He grabbed the keys and hurried out the door, leaving Miss Mama more than a bit surprised that Chatty didn't know how to use the keys to his own car.

ɷ

Across the road, Miss Alva hung up the kitchen phone, she explained the situation to Pepper.

"I need to get these casseroles in the oven. I'll stir up the caramel icing for the cake while the layers bake." From the fridge, she removed dishes with her special sour cream potatoes and macaroni and cheese."

Miss Alva was extremely intuitive and sensitive to others. She had fine-tuned the skills as a politician's wife, though she also had to learn to cap it when it came to criticism of her husband. McCager Burnett had a temper like a wild cat, so he handled himself quite well while his wife looked on with pride. Though she was working with her back to Pepper, she could feel his anxiety. He wanted to see Stella as soon as possible.

"May I help you in any way?" he asked.

"Would you like to head on over to Martha Annie's in your four-wheel drive, then come back and get me in about an hour?"

His face lit up. Just before he said "Yes," he remembered that he had not yet met Stella's mama, so he felt a bit awkward. Especially after Miss Alva had told him that the Governor and Stella were in the barn with a horse about to deliver. Stella wouldn't be there to make it any easier for him when he got to the home.

It was hard to say but he forced the words out. "No ma'am, I'll just wait until you're ready to leave." He tried to turn it into a joke. "Miss Alva, the Governor would never forgive me for leaving you alone in this kind of weather. I'm a law enforcement officer. I know better and he knows I know better." Pepper then chuckled, half-heartedly.

Miss Alva nodded and smiled. "Thank you."

She pretended she didn't know better. "I hope we can leave by five when it starts getting dark. We had planned to have a late breakfast at Martha Annie's, but had to change plans."

Behind her back, Pepper slipped a look at his watch. Three-thirty. Another ninety minutes before he could see Stella's alluring green eyes.

☙

Melissa continued to be uncomfortable. She said nothing to Daniel because she didn't want to worry him. By 4:20 p.m., she had no choice. The pain was becoming more intense.

"Daniel," she called from the bedroom. "I'm not real sure but… I think I may be havin' labor pains."

"Sweetie, you're not due for another two weeks." They were both brand new to this experience.

"Just in case, maybe we should call Dr. Colby. His number's by the phone."

As Daniel was frantically dialing, so nervous that he kept hitting a wrong number, the lights flickered twice. They'd be out any time now. But finally, he got through to Dr. Colby, who had thoughtfully given them his cell number.

"She couldn't be in labor now, could she?" Daniel asked the doctor.

"Predicting a baby's arrival isn't an exact science. In fact, we rarely get the exact date correct. The good Lord's in charge of that. It's His will that's done, not ours. Now, what I want you to do is keep her calm, but have her tell you every time she has a sharp pain. Time the length between the pains. You've got a thirty-five mile drive to the hospital and, in this weather, it's gonna take much longer. When her pains are eight minutes apart, call me back. Normally, we'd wait until about four minutes, but not in this weather. Do you have a four-wheel drive vehicle?"

"Yes, sir. My service truck."

"Very good. Call me back in an hour and we'll see what to do from there."

A few minutes before five, there was no question. The bed was soaked with water.

Chapter Nine

Daniel's face turned the whitest of whites. Melissa gently patted his hand. "Sweetheart, it's okay. Women been doin' this for thousands of years. Just pray for me." He knelt by the bed and begged for God's grace. Strength was draining from Melissa's body. She could barely speak. As Daniel dug the phone number from his jacket pocket, Melissa closed her eyes and thought of what Dr. Colby had cautioned her the previous day in his office.

"Child birthin' takes a lot outta a woman. Now, I don't mean this unkindly but you're not a young woman. It's gonna be a struggle, I 'pect." He shrugged, running a hand through his thick white hair. He looked at the white linoleum floor, thinking on what he was going to say and just how he was going to say it.

He thought a few seconds too long and Melissa became nervous. "Doctor, what you are aiming to say to me?"

He cleared his throat. "I'm thinkin' we might do a cesarean. Perhaps that baby's been growin' quite a bit in the last couple of weeks. I think you're tall enough to be fine, but you've always been too thin." Melissa was happy that Daniel was in there until he had to step out in the waiting room to take a call from the office. He was worried enough already, and his worry was making her nervous. After some more thinking and checking everything again, Dr. Colby rubbed his chin and realized he hadn't shaved this morning because he rushed to the hospital to check on his mamas and babies since the hospital was anxious to release as many well or nearly-well patients before the strong snowfall that was expected the next day. The previous day, Dr. Colby met the Madisons at the hospital then made up his mind; Melissa was going home. Maybe she'd have the baby at home.

The doctor looked at Melissa. "I've half a mind to keep you here. What with yu'uns livin' up in those foothills."

"You're from there, too," Melissa winked. "Us mountain folks stick together, don't we?"

That gave the doctor an idea.

"You live close to that old codger, McCager Burnett, isn't that right?"

"Why surely we do, and he ain't an old codger," she said, firmly. "Finest man I ever knowed and Miss Alva, she's been real good to us, too. Cooks for us when she's home since I've been in this condition." She rubbed her belly lovingly through the red top she was wearing.

He chuckled. "I went to school from first grade on with Cage in Turniptown, over the mountain from you. We've been best friends ever since."

She pushed a blonde piece of hair behind her ear. "I never knowed that."

"Finest friend I've had 'cept for the time he got himself elected Governor. The first thing he did was appoint me to a state medical board. Took so much of my dadgum time and never got paid one red cent." He shook his head and grinning. "I'd do anything for Cage. Anything."

Melissa wasn't one bit fooled that he had ever been annoyed by being appointed to board.

"Some friendship y'all must have. Especially if you growed up with him." She smiled. Melissa was known for her smile. "He must trust you a lot. I've only knowed them a few years and I seen how McCager Burnett does not suffer fools."

Chuckling, Dr. Colby sat down and folded his arms across his white jacket, saying "And Cagey, like he's called by everyone he ever outsmarted, especially in Washington, D.C—and there've many—loves to see fools suffer. The bigger the fool, the more entertaining it is for him." He gave her a cheerful wink.

Back to serious thinking, he went with his mind, chewing his lower lip. It was an inherited habit from his daddy. And as he studied on the situation, she smiled at him. One reason she and Daniel chose Dr. Colby for their baby doctor was he talked mountain like they did and, despite graduating first in his medical class and having his choice of high falutin' hospitals, he wanted to doctor at the hospital nearest to his people.

Weathermen get things as wrong as lawyers or doctors. In fact, weathermen err on the wrong side more often than not. So, maybe they were wrong again this time. Dr. Colby reached up and took down a funeral home calendar from the wall.

"Funeral home?" Melissa asked, nervously, as he flipped the front over. "You don't use one like this? Shows the signs of the moon. Picked it up over the mountain during a visitation," Dr. Colby said.

"My granny plants her garden accordin' to the signs." Melissa nodded. "And when turnip season and collar greens time git here, she follows it to the spec. All the truck farmers want her greens to take down to the Atlanta Farmer's Market."

"Smart woman, your granny. A person has to be mighty careful to stir up a batch of "sour" kraut, as our people call it, on the right time of moon or it'll turn bad. Real bad. Bad shore 'nuff."

There was a small knock on the door. "Kin I come back in?" whispered Daniel.

"C'mon in." The doc was hanging the calendar back on the wall and Daniel raised one eyebrow.

"We got us anything to worry 'bout?" Worry filled Daniel's blue eyes.

"No, siree," answered Dr. Colby, turning around with a smile. "The way I sees it, what you need to be worryin' about is earning 'nuff money to feed that big baby you got who's growin' by the minute. Whew."

Daniel's lips stretched into an enormous grin. "Big 'un, huh?" He shook his head happily then hugged Melissa's tightly.

"Sorry 'bout that phone call. Since the bad weather's comin', my boss wants to know if I can help out. And I said it depends on what y'all were sayin' in here."

"She can't wait until her due date. That child needs out."

Daniel threw his hands atop his head, and held them there, while he looked back and forth between the doctor and his wife's sweet face. Fifteen years married after four years a-courtin' and finally they were gonna see that precious baby they'd had every church, all over the mountains, praying for. Their prayers were about to be answered.

The doctor held a hand. "Whoa! Not so quick, Danny Boy!"

"You said 'it's big' and 'can't wait until the due date'."

"The baby's big enough. Well enough. And ready. But mama's not ready. It could be a few days or more. The baby's about seven and a half pounds. If he or she gets too close to nine, Melissa may not be able to have the baby naturally. And, like you said, bad weather's comin'."

Bewildered, Daniel shook his head. "What's this you's sayin?"

"We'd have to do a cesarean."

Melissa smiled real big. "That sounds easier."

The doctor put his hand on her arm. "Easier at the time but not as easy to recover from, especially while caring for a new baby. Also, C-section babies sometimes tend to have more sickness and, sometimes, they'll carry it with them on down through the journey of life such as acid reflux or other stomach problems."

Daniel's brow furrowed. "Why's that?"

"Son, the good Lord was right smart 'bout how He made all of nature. Right now, you're lookin' at one of His works of nature—a fragile woman who's spent close to nine months creating this baby that all your people have been prayin' for. And she's done everything I asked. But the gracious Almighty has given Miss Melissa all she needs to deliver this baby. Women did this a long time without doctors. Who do you reckon delivered Cain and Abel? Occasionally, us doctors are needed for various reasons, none of which I see here. The baby's well-positioned. And that's an excellent sign. So, at this point, the only reason for a C-Section is if it gets too big." Dr. Colby smiled.

Daniel and Melissa were listening intently. "You mentioned he might be sickly? Maybe for a lifetime?" There was no smile in Melissa's eyes. Only worry.

"Daniel, you gather 'round with us." Daniel moved closer to the examining chair while the doctor twisted the knob on the side and set Melissa upright from the lounging position, on the previous day.

"You weren't here when your wife and I talked about whether to give mother's milk or formula."

"No, sir. But she done told me all 'bout it and the good advice you gave her. No two ways about it, strictly mama's milk." Melissa and Daniel smiled at each other lovingly and held hands. Dr. Colby walked to a rack of brochures and pulled one out. Standing, facing them, he said, "This brochure is about breast feeding. If you look all the way down at the reasons—I don't know how many, twenty or twenty five—optimal nutrition, reduced risk of disease, brain improvement." The doctor nudged Daniel with a grin. "Now, ya want 'im to be smarter than you, right?"

Daniel was laughing. "Ain't no way. But, beg your pardon, we done decided on this." Melissa was nodding firmly. "We already got us a machine so Melissa can put her milk in a bottle to take to church or other places where's it's more appropriate." Mountain folks are gentle with their language. Most of them.

"This has nothin' to do with a C-Section? Or I'm 'bout to get plenty nervous?" Daniel said as he began chewing on a hangnail.

The doctor laughed. "Does take me awhile when I get to talkin' about medicine and how the good Lord designed things. A child that's born naturally, through the birth canal, takes in good bacteria, called flora, from his mama. The mama's bacteria covers the baby's skin and even gets inside his intestines. Babies born by C-section don't get some of those Lord's special gifts."

Daniel and Melissa looked at one another, again. Then, after a moment, Dr. Colby said, "Tell you what—I'm gonna make a decision for you. You can change it up later if you've a mind to, but I'm the doctor. Now, the hospital's closin' for the snow comin' so it'll be goin' to a skeleton crew. I thought about keepin' you here but that's a sorry way to spend Christmas in my opinion. You aren't showin' any signs of a woman fixin' to give birth soon but since its weight is startin' to concern, yu'uns come by the day after Christmas. If there's a need then, or any kind of change, I can induce labor and, hopefully, the baby will take a nudge and hurry on out."

He watched them as he looked out the window, huddled together, walking to the parking lot. He thought of all the babies he had delivered. He stopped counting at nine hundred and sixty-one because, all a-sudden, it made him sad to think that a good bit of his practice was behind him. There was something precious about that couple. He had given them his private cell phone number, the one he answered when a baby was coming, and told them to carry it. If they weren't neighbors with McCager and Alva Burnett, he would have taken a second think on letting them go, but McCager could commandeer a state helicopter if needed.

Dr. Colby lit his pipe as he watched Daniel comically trying to put his wife in the four-wheel drive truck. Out loud, he whispered, "Seein' those two happy is all the Christmas present I want. Thank you, Lord."

ꝏ

Had that all just happened yesterday? Melissa was thinking about all of it, every word the doctor had said. If labor began before Friday, he would have a law car, lights flashing, get him to the hospital. McCager, he had promised, would take care of Melissa. He had his own law connections, too. She was trying to stay calm because Daniel was pacing the kitchen. She could see him from where she laid on the soaking bed. He repeatedly kept punching his cell phone.

"Honey," Melissa called weakly, "Is there a problem?"

"No, darlin', no problem." But he was shaking all over. He knew his phone never had more than two bars on it, and usually just one, and it worked. Now, he had no signal. He heard a powerful cracking and looked out the kitchen window in time to see an oak tree charging toward the ground. Working for the forestry made Daniel good at judging the depth of snow.

"Oh, no," he whispered. "Ten inches of snow. There won't be no service between here and the hospital."

Then, he whispered a prayer.

Chapter Ten

Daniel decided it was time to figure out the best solution. It was a little past five with a dark winter's sky that was brightened significantly by the pile of snow. With the darkness, there would be a steep drop in temperature. Before he could make the thirty-five mile drive to the hospital, the snow would have a layer of ice on it. Also, trees, power and phone lines would be falling while teenagers would be sliding into other cars and into gullies. Tonight, he and the good Lord had to be in charge and make the right decision. Melissa and he had been waiting for this little one for too many years.

The thought came to him suddenly: McCager Burnett. Dr. Colby's last words were, "If you need help, call Cage. He can get a state trooper helicopter." He was starting to feel the zing of enthusiasm return. The Governor was over at the Jackson farm. He'd take Melissa over there and follow the Governor's best advice. But just as he put the period on that sentence, Melissa let out a scream the likes of which he had never heard. It scared him to death.

In socked feet, he slid down the hallway and straight to her bed. Her face was flush, and she was trying to hold back tears.

"Daniel, it's the worst pain I've ever felt." Another holler. "Did you get Dr. Colby on the phone?"

He took a deep breath and knelt beside her, taking her hand, "Missy, don't you worry. Not for one second. Me and the Lord have you and everything will be fine."

Melissa paid serious attention to another "calling card" from their child then looked at Daniel, worriedly, "You can't get Dr. Colby on the phone?"

She knew Daniel Madison too well. He didn't have to utter a word. Tears dripped off her cheek. "Danny, I'm scared."

He took charge. "Baby, can you sit up if I help you?" Forgetting that he was wearing socks on a shiny wood floor, it didn't do real well with the mommy, baby, and extra girth. "Melissa, sit right here while I git my shoes, the hospital bag, and our coats."

"I need my high-top farm boots." He looked down at her bedroom shoes. "Yes, honey, you do. I'll get those, too."

Daniel scrambled through the house, grabbing the suitcase from the living room and their coats and hats from the tree stand. Helping Melissa put on her boots and coat, she let out another scream. They were both nervous wrecks but not so much that Melissa didn't remember her purse.

"It's on the kitchen table," she said between the pains. "I need my insurance card." She smiled faintly. "And my lipstick. I want to look pretty in our first picture."

Daniel looked back at Melissa and winked. "Good thinking." He'd do anything to get her spirits up. "I'm gonna carry this stuff out to the truck then come back for the prettiest girl in Turner's Corner."

She tried to smile. "Stella's home. But I don't mind bein' second best."

Daniel was headed out the door, plum loaded down. "The carrier, baby blanket, and safety seat. Don't forget those."

Melissa nodded pitifully. She had planned so well—but not on a bloomin', foot-high blizzard.

"Don't worry," he called. "I'll git 'em." Fifteen minutes later, Daniel had everything thrown in the back seat of the extended-cab truck. He patted the hood as he walked by. "This is gonna be the most important event in the life of a Ford 350 service truck belonging to the United States Government. Great county to be born in, son." He ran up the two steps, into the kitchen, glancing at his watch. Over fifty minutes since the baby had announced his forthcoming arrival by soaking the bed. Daniel swallowed hard and tried to get ahold of himself.

"Danny, tell me honest—can we make it?"

"I can promise we will for two big reasons. The Man up there and the two men down here."

After another scream, she looked puzzled, so Daniel explained. "Jesus is watchin 'over us, up there, and McCager is over, at the Jackson farm, and that's where I'll take you, first."

It was the first look of relief that Daniel had seen on her face. Gingerly, with his arms tight around her, he helped Melissa down the hallway, then down the steps to the carport, making sure she didn't slip. He then opened the passenger's side door. "Danny, I won't be able to lift my leg up, on the runnin' board. It's always been challenging,' but now..." He rubbed his chin and looked around.

"Thank you, buddy," he said to Melissa's swollen stomach. It was a tiny, faded blue plastic child's stool that Daniel had bought for a dollar at a yard sale. "You're already helpin' on the farm." Daniel was making conversation while he was working hard on not dropping his wife.

Once he had Melissa up, in the truck, they both looked at each wearily before he broke into a big grin. "Mama, it's all gonna be worth it. Not much longer and it'll be over. Like my granddaddy always said, 'There's a better day a-comin'." As Daniel ran to the driver's side, he could hear the loud crunch of his boots on the ice already.

Concerned, he glanced heavenward. "I know you won't let us down."

ଋ

The electricity went off at the Governor and Miss Alva's house just as she took out the last casserole. The caramel cake was iced and ready to go, already in Miss Alva's favorite cake carrier.

"Oh, dear," she said. "Next to that kitchen door is McCager's big barn light. Would you get it, please?"

"Yes, ma'am," Pepper said in a nicer way than he felt. Somehow, leaving at five had turned into five thirty. Now, this was liable to set them back another couple of handfuls of minutes. Alva stood on tiptoes and pointed to a short cabinet above the 'fridge.

"Pepper, let me hold the flashlight while you, please, get those two flat navy lids? They're for the casserole dishes. Then, tell you what. You go and warm your car while I wrap these dishes in newspaper and towels and put them in a basket."

"Good thing I'm parked under your carport or we'd never get that snow and ice off."

"Pepper, let's take that flashlight to make sure we don't make a mis-step." Pepper's SUV wasn't quite so high off the ground (plus she wasn't carrying a big baby), and that made things much easier for Miss Alva.

"Whew, what an adventure this day has been," Miss Alva said. "I wonder how Chatty is doing in these primitive woods. Did I hear someone mention that he's brought that poor, beleaguered Spencer, his butler, along with silver and china?"

"Don't forget those expensive sheets he brags on all the time."

She turned and stared at Pepper. "Porthault?" She shook her head. "He's been worrying that heaven will be a letdown for him after his life here, on earth!"

"Is he sure he's going to make it there?" They laughed as Pepper kept his eye on the drive.

"Isn't it pretty here with the clean snow, a full moon rising, and silence?" Miss Alva asked with the awe of someone seeing the mountains for the first time. "I am certainly glad that Melissa Madison's baby isn't due for another couple of weeks. It'd be awful trying to get to the hospital in this kind of weather."

Pepper pulled to the end of the drive and chuckled. "I'm glad they live just across the road and no other cars are sliding around. It's hard to see."

"I'll direct you. McCager says I'm pretty good at that," she joked. "Turn onto the road, here. The Madisons' mailbox is about fifty yards down, then Sims and Martha Annie's is about twenty feet past that—but, of course, on the other side of the road."

Just then, Miss Alva's eyes caught red taillights sticking up, from a pile of snow, along the side of the road. She clutched Pepper's arm. "Pepper, someone's had a wreck." Seeing this, he slowly pulled closer only to see the emblem of the U.S. Forestry Service on the door.

Pepper grabbed his marshal's badge off the dash then turned on the red and blue flashing strobes along with the high beam headlights.

"Miss Alva, I'm afraid it's the Madisons. Stay right here."

It was the driver's side that had gone in the ditch. The passenger's side was facing up. With a gloved hand, Pepper cleared the window and pressed his badge against it. Melissa nodded and let down the window.

"I'm United States Marshal Culpepper. Are you Mrs. Madison?"

"Yes. Marshal, I'm in labor. We had no phone service, and my husband was in a hurry, as you can see," she grunted.

"Where is he now?"

"He climbed out the back. He's walking to Sims and Martha Annie's. The Governor's over there. Maybe he can help. And she has a landline so we can call the doctor."

"Would you be willing to let me transfer you to my car? Miss Alva's in there. We're on our way over there, too."

She nodded.

Pepper opened the back door on the SUV, then the passenger door of the truck. "Are you able to put your arms around my neck?"

"I think so."

With her arms around his neck, Pepper's left arm behind her back, and his right arm beneath her legs, the marshal slowly lifted her out of the truck. The transfer into his car went easily and he winked, "I believe you're the lightest pregnant woman I've rescued."

"I'll take the compliment, thank you."

As Miss Alva made over Melissa, checking to see that she wasn't hurt, Pepper turned into Stella's drive.

A good ways past the old farm truck that Bubba had decorated with lights for Stella, they saw Daniel Madison trudging through the deep snow, edging closer to the farmhouse, exhausted. Pepper stopped the SUV as Miss Alva put down the window.

"Melissa's with us. Hop in the back, Daniel."

What a Christmas Eve this was turning out to be.

Chapter Eleven

Bubba came back from the fourth feeding stall, puzzled. He had a habit of reaching behind his ear and scratching his neck when he was studying on something that didn't make sense. He started to speak but he turned to look back at the stall.

Shaking his head and still lost in thought, he said, "Sweet feed 'round here keeps goin' a-missin'. For two weeks, maybe more. I keep movin' it and the dang thing, whatever it is, finds it." Then, with a shrug, "Whatever's gettin' that feed sure has a big appetite."

Chatty had gone to retrieve his "simply marvelous" Christmas decorations.

The Governor cracked, "I believe this might be the first perfectly decorated Christmas barn. Leastways, around here." He thought on it for a moment as he leaned against the wall separating the first two stalls, one leg slung casually over the other, the tip of his knee-high boot resting on the concrete floor. With both hands thrust deep into the pockets of his three-quarter length barn coat, McCager looked perfectly placed. Yet, he was a man who could play in both worlds and hold his own without giving up his authentic self. The grand portrait that hung in the marbled state capitol, to celebrate his two terms of his Governorship, demonstrated powerfully who McCager Burnett was. While other past governors posed alone, Cager insisted that Miss Alva be in the portrait, as well.

"Us mountain folks are loyal. I know who got me where I am and it's this fine woman. She's stood behind me all the way." Thus, McCager's portrait features him, wearing a nice suit, sitting in a leather chair, with Miss Alva standing behind him. Just like always.

On this day, he was the mountain man he was born to be, keenly observing all the goings on, when he thought of his old friend, Sims Jackson. And that brought forth a laugh. "What do reckon ol' Sims would say about havin' a $75,000 horse in his barn? And it's about to be finely decorated, too." McCager winked. "It would do my old heart good if the great Almighty would pull back the veil tonight and let Sims see this farm, covered in snow and decorations from the most expensive store in Atlanta. Stella girl, what would he say about that?"

"That we've gotten above our raisin' and that he'd learned us better."

Bubba was hunched down in the stall, hand-feeding sweet feed to Fancy Sadie. "Boy, do I miss that old guy. He taught me so much. Stella, you were the brave one. You marched right out of these hills and down to Atlanta. You wound up in the center of wealth and mansions."

Stella blushed. Bubba knew well the story of her downfall, in the most public of ways, and how she, covered in shame, had run straight back to her beloved mountains when it happened. She whispered to herself, disappointed, "Whole lotta good it did me."

Bubba stood up, followed by Fancy Sadie. Big Black stuck his head through the window to remind them all that he was the grand stallion and the father of the foal to be born. As Bubba fed the remainder of the sweet feed to Big Black, he said, "Stellie, you might want to go inside and call Lynn and Ronnie with an update."

"Of course. What should I tell them?"

"That it looks like Sadie's starting her labor."

ꝏ

Carefully, Pepper eased his SUV up the road to the Jackson farmhouse where their power had not gone out yet, but it was certainly only a matter of time. Probably minutes. It was still well-lighted with indoor lamps as well as festive lights wrapped around porch posts, outlining the front door and a Christmas tree, in the front window, glowing with red, green and blue old-fashioned lights. Martha Annie had been using those same lights since the first year she and Sims were married. In the short time that Stella was somewhat of an Atlanta socialite—she was never fully accepted but was more of a "faux socialite"—Stella had bought boxes of new decorations, and more modern, tiny white lights, to give the old farmhouse a Yule Tide facelift.

But her mama was having none of it. "You just put them right back in your car and tote them back to Atlanta. I'm plenty pleased with what I got. I don't need no fancy stuff. Why, what would the folks at church say? They'd say, 'Martha Annie Jackson's got too big for her britches'."

"But Mama," Stella had started to make her case.

"Don't 'But Mama' me. I'm puttin' my foot down."

Martha Annie had then walked over to the old kitchen sink where she washed dishes, daily, beginning sixty-five years ago since she never had a dishwasher. In the windowsill set two small pots of aloe vera that were used if someone's finger got burned. Breaking one of the thick, velvet-like leaves in half, it oozed a gel that would immediately ease the throb. Martha Annie stared out the window at the grand oak tree that stood providing shade from the afternoon sun for both the kitchen and the porch, where a two-person swing hung and two rocking chairs, built by Sims' grandfather, rested on either side of the door. After a long moment of reminiscing how Sims had proposed on that swing, and where she had often rocked her two daughters in her arms, Martha Annie picked up the corner of her blue checked apron and dabbed at her eyes.

Alarmed, Stella gently put her arm around her mama's shoulders and asked softly, "What's wrong? What is it?"

"Stella, you can't just take a person's happy remembrances away so easily. Every day, I watch the happiness of days gone by, disappearing little by little. Sims is buried in the church graveyard and both of my girls have gone off to have lives of their own. I don't even have grandchildren. If it weren't for Bubba and Rooster, I'd be mostly alone. I cling to as much of what's left as I possibly can." She turned to her daughter. "You remember that big maple on the back side of the property, near the creek?"

Stella nodded and smiled at the thought of their summer suppers on the ground beneath its massive limbs. "The one with our childhood swing."

Martha Annie nodded. "It uprooted in the last steady rainstorm. It had rained for days. And the ground was so soft that it couldn't take the weight. Bubba and Rooster spent the better part of three days cutting it up into firewood."

Stella's green eyes sprang open with surprise. "Mama!" she exclaimed, her heart filled with a huge dose of sadness, "Why didn't you tell me?" Stella and Lynn had played there almost daily, taking turns pushing each other on a tire swing that Sims had put up while standing in the back of his truck. With help from Rooster, Sims slung the rope over a tall limb and tied it good. And there were other times, they waded in the creek, watching tadpoles or rescuing small turtles who crawled too close to the edge.

"I couldn't," she replied. "It was too sad to think about and I shore couldn't talk 'bout it.

At that moment, Stella understood. Those old Christmas lights represented a time when Martha Annie's life was satisfying, and their family was all together with no unsettling interruptions from death or empty bedrooms. When Stella returned on a visit from Atlanta, she brought along a large box of the big bulbs.

"Here you go, mama," Stella said, smiling. "Bulbs to replace any of the others that burn out. This ought to do you for a few years, at least."

Martha Annie pushed a wisp of gray hair out of her eyes and smiled happily. "These oughta do me 'til the good Lord calls me home." She hugged her daughter tightly, meaningfully.

"Just make sure you have Rooster check all the wiring. We don't want an electrical fire."

So, this was how Pepper saw Stella's childhood home for the first time, amidst the snow-covered trees and mountains and Christmas lights. Though the two-story clapboard was a hundred years old, it looked like a Currier and Ives print. Pepper slowed to a crawl so he could take it all in. To him, it was lovelier than any home he had ever seen in Memphis, Graceland withstanding. A wail of agony jarred him, reminding him of the assignment at hand. He pressed the gas pedal slightly. Arriving at the house, he discovered there was no garage. And blocking an easy way to the nearest door was an older farm truck, a sedan that probably belonged to Mrs. Jackson, the Governor's ten-year-old truck that stayed at the farm, Stella's car, and an enormous vehicle covered by snow but was probably another SUV.

Pepper put his car in park, looked over at Miss Alva, then glanced in back to Daniel sitting directly behind her, cradling Melissa in his arms. "Mr. Madison, what should we do now?"

Daniel Madison was so aflutter that he couldn't think and could barely force words out. "I don't know. I don't know." He was about to start wailing like Melissa but, as though a switch had suddenly been flipped, he took hold of himself. Though they were both frightened of losing the baby they'd wanted for so many years, Daniel realized that he was the man of the house, and he had to take care of his family. In an amazingly quick turn of emotion, he calmly said, "Let's pray."

Miss Alva peeped around her seat so she could look him directly in the eye and smiled her approval. "Wonderful idea."

All bowed their heads and Melissa's crying stopped for a moment as Daniel asked for guidance in their decision as to how to save both mother and child. When he said, "Amen," the group was silent for a moment. Then, with renewed strength and calm, Daniel said, "First, I need to call Dr. Colby. I'll go inside and use Miss Martha Annie's landline."

"No!" Melissa cried out. "Please, don't leave."

The always level-headed Alva Burnett said, "Daniel, why don't you give me his number and I'll call? McCager and I go way back with George Colby."

Daniel dug into his shirt pocket, handed Miss Alva a piece of paper with the number written on it, and thanked her.

"Let me help you so you won't slip and fall," Pepper said.

"Pepper, I'm mountain born and raised. This isn't the first big snowstorm or emergency I've faced." She patted his hand. "You stay with the Madisons." Still, Pepper watched her closely until he saw she was safely on the porch. Though the light was dim and even flickered a few times, he saw Miss Alva stop for a moment to speak with someone before pulling open the screen door and entering. The person she'd spoken to hurried out, to the back of the enormous vehicle parked in front of them. He was strangely attired, pressing a key fob, opening the trunk, and shaking off the little bit of snow that fell off. His pants, tucked in, ballooned over knee-high boots, like riding plants. He wore an old black coat with a tear on the left sleeve. Atop his head was a red, knit stocking cap with a short tail at the end of which hung a green pom-pom.

Something about him and the way he moved seemed familiar as he pulled a large wreath and two boxes from the trunk, fumbling them briefly before stacking them on top of one other. Apparently finished, he took his haul back to the porch then returned to pull down the trunk lid. Yet, regardless of how hard he tugged, the lid didn't seem to budge.

Pepper closed his eyes and shook his head. There could be only one person, within a thousand miles, who walked like that, who bumbled like that, who'd have an expensive car like that—who was clueless about how to close the trunk.

Chatham Balsam Colquitt IV.

Pepper tooted the horn once and flashed his lights. Chatty put up his hand to shield his eyes and peered toward the vehicle. Lowering his window halfway, Pepper called out, "Hey, Chatty. Press the button and it will go down by itself."

It took Chatty a moment to find the button but when he did, the lid began slowly lowering, and his hands flew to cover his mouth as his eyes widened, astounded at what he was seeing. After the trunk closed with a click, Chatty hurried over to Pepper.

"I've never seen such technology!"

"You also don't know how to dial out on your cell phone, only how to answer it. You might be surprised what all you'd learn if you expanded your horizons."

"Horizons? Such as? Never mind." Chatty waved away this kind of nonsense. "Pepper, how many times must I persist in telling you that it is not incumbent upon me to clutter my mind. I have money. Copious amounts of money, so I have people who can do whatever I needeth doing."

"Well, Shakespeare, you'd have been stuck this time, for I spy none of your people in attendance."

Chatty motioned toward the farmhouse. "Spencer, my butler, is helping Miss Mama in the kitchen."

"Miss Mama?"

Melissa shrieked in pain at that moment, causing Chatty to jump back in horror, declaring what all women in strong labor want to hear, "I *knew* there were wild animals out here! I should have stayed on Sea Island where we have guards at the gate and it's safe."

Pepper put his head back, against the headrest. He didn't know how to begin explaining all of this, saying, "Chatty, do I really need to tell you about the birds and the bees?"

Chapter Twelve

Alva Burnett didn't bother to knock on Martha Annie's inside door. She simply announced herself as she marched right in. This was no time to practice formality.

Martha Annie hugged her dear friend, "Merry Christmas!"

Again, forsaking convention, Miss Alva said, "I need to use your phone. It's an emergency."

Alarmed, but knowing it was no time for questions, she replied, "Stella's on the phone with Lynn. We have one of their horses and she's about to foal a bit early. Let me ask Stella to call Lynn back."

Of course, the first thing that crossed Martha Annie's mind was something was wrong with Cager, but it couldn't be that because he was in the barn with Bubba. Alva followed her friend into the kitchen, then blinked when she saw Spencer, whom she knew from their many dinners and soirees at Chatty's when they were all in Atlanta and not on Sea Island.

"Spencer! What're you doing spending Christmas in the backwoods of Georgia?"

"Mr. Colquitt requested I accompany him. We brought his finest china and silver."

Miss Alva smiled and shook her head with the emotions of both love and amusement. It was one of the reasons that the Burnetts adored Chatty. He was never dull, always amusing, and often quite unpredictable.

"Excuse me, madam, while I return to preparing sandwiches and nibbles in the event the power should cease."

"Purely out of curiosity, have you ever been in a house when the power is out?"

"No, madam. Mr. Colquitt has two generators to ensure we are never powerless."

Just like Chatty. Always over the top. Why have one generator when you could have two? Something the Burnetts understood that no one, including his adored Stella, realized about Chatham Balsam Colquitt IV was that he was orphaned as a teenager. And except for a few distant cousins, he had no family and no one to inherit his vast fortune. Though he was often pretentious about his wealth, he actually had no idea how much money, property, and stocks he had. The Governor was his estate attorney and he had always thought it best that Chatty didn't know the degree of his wealth—only that he could afford whatever he wanted. Otherwise, he would own a private jet and an island in the South Pacific.

He had recently updated his will, at McCager's insistance, designating generous amounts to the long-suffering Spencer and his Sea Island butler, Bailey, as well as much smaller amounts to his chefs and housekeepers, reasoning that they were all young enough to continue working for a living.

"I believe everyone should work for their income unless they are born into wealth, created by others, who worked to earn it." Typical Chatty reasoning. McCager refused Chatty's declaration to put the Burnetts in his will because, as the Governor said, "First, we don't need the money. Second, in all likelihood, you will outlive us. And third, and most importantly, it would be unethical, a conflict of interests since I'm the one writing your will."

"Then, I want all that remains to go to my Stella." The Governor had smiled and nodded. The love that Chatty had for Stella was pure, unvarnished adoration.

"Have you considered leaving an endowment to your church? I'm quite certain the Presbyterians would appreciate it."

Chatty's expression turned to quizzical. "Why should I do that? God has much more money than I do."

The Governor dropped his head and rubbed his forehead. Chatty's reasoning was unique. Just like Chatty.

"Besides, I know Stellie will give generously, enormously, to anyone in need," Chatty said, sitting back in his chair. And just like that, as was so often the case, Chatty had redeemed himself.

ᏧᏒ

Martha Annie slipped Stella a note that Miss Alva needed the phone. Stella held up her forefinger and nodded to signal she would wrap it up, quickly.

"There's no way that Dr. Milo could get here. It's a blizzard. Between Bubba, the Governor, and me, we should be able to handle it. I'll keep you posted. Miss Alva is here, and she needs to use the phone. Talk to you later. Miss you, love you."

Stella handed the phone to Miss Alva who kissed Stella on the cheek. She immediately began pushing buttons on the wall phone. And just as she hit the last number, the power went out. Martha Annie, quick on the draw, began lighting the kerosene lamps, including two lanterns to take to the barn, and several large candles.

"Quite interesting," commented Spencer. "Mrs. Jackson, shall I duct tape the oven door now?" Stella and Miss Alva blinked, but said not a word.

In just a few hours, a gentleman's gentleman from London was learning quite a lot in the piney woods of the Appalachians. Stella tucked her big flashlight under her arm, took a lantern in each hand, and headed out the door while her mama held it open.

As Martha Annie closed the door, she heard Miss Alva say, "Hello, George? This is Alva Burnett. Yes,

I'm fine and McCager is, too. Merry Christmas to you and Betty. I realize it's unusual to hear from me, especially on Christmas Eve, but here's the situation."

Miss Alva explained quickly then listened to his response. "George, I'd have to agree with you. It's dark and ice is already forming on top of the snow. It would be dangerous, even foolhardy, even to try. In fact, the Madisons were barely out of the driveway before they slid off the road."

Martha Annie, usually unflappable, was so stunned that she stopped duct taping the oven. She was trying to think what on earth they were going to do.

On the other end of the line, Dr. George Colby was attempting to reassure Miss Alva.

"I can talk y'all through this."

"George, I've never had a child, but we're at our neighbor's house and she has had two. That's the positive. The negative is that the electricity's gone off and all we have are kerosene lamps and candles."

George Colby was used to soothing nervous mothers-to-be, however, even after forty years of practicing, this was a new one for him. He thought quickly. "Alva, millions of babies were born by candlelight and kerosene lamp. And you're more fortunate since you have a working phone line and me to talk you through it. Now, get Melissa in the house and into a comfortable, warm bed with clean sheets."

"Do we boil water?" she asked, causing the doctor to spontaneously laugh.

"As a matter of fact, that would be a fine idea," he replied. "Holding a warm compresses on her belly would soothe the pain. And keeping a wet cloth on her forehead will be comforting. But you're out of power. Do you have a gas range to boil water?"

Alva glanced over to the stove and saw that it was electric. "Do we have any way to boil water?" she asked Martha Annie who thought for a moment then had an idea. She nodded and mouthed the single word, "Yes."

"We do!" Alva exclaimed. It was a triumph she needed.

"Wonderful, Alva. Just stay calm so Melissa will stay calm. It's very important. Be reassuring. You and McCager have been in more troubling situations than this, so draw your strength from those times. Call me back when you have Melissa inside and settled."

Alva hung up the phone and looked at Martha Annie. "We're about to deliver a baby," she said calmly, just as George Colby had instructed.

ଓ

Pepper had barely finished explaining what all was happening amidst Melissa's moaning, when to Pepper's surprise, Chatty exclaimed, "That's what we're doing in the barn. We're birthing a baby!"

"A baby? In the barn?"

"Stella's sister is out of town and she left her expectant horse here." Chatty leaned closer to the open window and whispered, "The baby's father is here, too.

He's a big stallion that cost $75,000!" Money always impressed Chatty. "Pepper, I'd love to stay and talk but I have to get Fancy Sadie's stall decorated for Christmas. Ciao!"

And off he stomped through the snow, leaving Pepper to process the idea that Chatty was going to decorate a barn stall. For a horse. As he watched Chatty marching in his ridiculous garb, he saw Miss Alva return, hurrying toward them, maneuvering the snow much better than Chatty. She opened the car door and climbed in.

"I talked to Dr. Colby and he's given us wise counsel. With his guidance, everything is going to be fine."

"What did he say?" Daniel asked, anxiously.

Miss Alva took a deep breath. "He believes we shouldn't chance an accident by driving to the hospital." Miss Alva heard two gasps from the back seat and turned to see tears running down Melissa's face. "Honey, it is all going to be fine. We won't let anything happen to you or your baby."

She handed a set of car keys to Pepper. "These are Chatty's. Would you, please, move his car so that we can drive closer to the door when we take Melissa in? Spencer wasn't appropriately attired to walk through a foot of snow." Miss Alva cut a sideward glance toward Pepper. "As you might imagine since Chatty dictates his wardrobe."

"Yes, ma'am." Pepper put his car in reverse and moved back enough to allow him to move Chatty's enormous vehicle, then he jumped out and hurriedly finished his task. Martha Annie was changing the sheets and boiling water. Their house was so old that a swinging, iron arm was built into the fireplace. She swung it out, built a fire, and hung the cast iron kettle filled with water. It was the "old-timey way" of doing things and she was glad she knew how to improvise.

Pepper's marshal training prepared him well, so, with his guidance, he and Daniel carried the suffering Melissa inside the house to Martha Annie's room since it was on the first floor. Miss Alva pulled Daniel aside and gave him strict instructions to remain calm, at least outwardly, because that would help keep Melissa calm.

"I'll do my best," he said. "But I'm awful nervous."

"To be completely honest, Daniel, so am I," Miss Alva replied then looked at him sternly. "But we can't let Melissa know that. Under no condition. Understood?"

He swallowed hard and nodded.

ଓ

Stella, arms loaded, kicked on the barn door a couple of times, and it was soon opened by the Governor who was carrying one of the three enormous flashlights they kept in the barn.

"Wonderful," he said. "We need more light."

"Let's just be careful with these lanterns. We don't want to kick one over and start a fire like Mrs. O'Leary's cow."

The Governor grinned and winked. "Good point. I saw a table in the corner. Let's move it near the stall and use the flashlights inside the stall."

She walked over to where Bubba was trying to gently quiet Fancy Sadie. He looked at Stella and shook his head.

"Poor girl. She's havin' a hard time of it. Whadda Lynn say?" Big Black had his head stuck through the window and he seemed to be watching Fancy Sadie with a fretful look in his eyes.

Stella shrugged. "She knows we're in a bad way but said just to do the best we can. She was very sweet and said she has faith in all of us. Ronnie's grandmother is edging toward the river Jordan. She shan't last long."

McCager Burnett, seasoned politician that he was, knew when courageous bravado was necessary. He also knew when to use his mountain talk. "Dadgum y'all, we's mountain folk. There ain't nothin' we can't do."

Stella gave him her most charmingly teasing smile. "Have you ever delivered a horse?"

"No. But I've delivered many a calf. And, I can tell you this, all God's creatures, both woman or beast, deliver the same way."

Neither of the men, of course, had any idea that, a short distance away, inside the house, a woman was going through labor pains just like Fancy Sadie.

Along with an anxious father watching—just as was Big Black.

Chapter Thirteen

When the trio heard another kick at the door, the Governor crossed again to answer it. There, he found Chatty, still wearing his sock hat, with a wreath slung around his neck and loaded down with four boxes. The stack was so high that only Chatty's warm brown eyes and the pom pom on his hat were visible.

McCager watched as Chatty, merrily singing *Jingle Bells*, set the boxes down on an old church pew that Sims Jackson had once rescued from a junk pile and refinished. Chatty sighed heavily.

"I have arrived later than I would've preferred but I had no light, so I had to take tiny steps and was very careful not to drop these boxes. That's the most manual labor that I've performed in quite a while."

"It's probably a fair assessment to say that it is the only manual labor you've ever done," remarked the Governor, eyeing Chatty without a smile. He was not being cruel or sarcastic. He was speaking only what he believed to be the truth. After all, he had known Chatty since he was born and his father had indulged Chatty with anything he desired, while Chatty's mother used the Colquitt wealth to jet around the world with Jackie

O. and her group of friends, including Truman Capote. In all fairness, though, she had not only married wealth, she had brought into the marriage three thousand acres of land and a slew of rental properties.

"You're doing that boy no favors," Cager had warned Chatham Balsam Colquitt III. "Life is not a fairy tale and he needs to learn that."

But McCager's words fell on deaf ears. Chatty was an only child who, by the age of three, had a vocabulary to rival some adults. He was precocious and quite entertaining. By the age of five, he was issuing orders to the house staff.

"It is pertinent that my bed be made to my liking," Chatty had once instructed a new housekeeper. "I simply cannot tolerate less. This, you must understand." He was six.

Rarely were all the Colquitts together. One parent or the other was always away. His father was a lawyer. His mother? An active participant in the joys of life. Usually, it was his mother who put her enjoyment over the upbringing of her son. When his parents, returning from the Belmont Stakes, had perished in a private plane crash, it had fallen upon the Burnetts to break the news. Miss Alva, whose heart was enormously tender toward Chatty, had cried for days over the devastation Chatty felt. But since he was accustomed to absent parents, he bounced back rather quickly. McCager, though regarded as tough and downright ornery, was equally pained for Chatty. They wrapped their loving arms around Chatty and brought him into their family.

Though he was old enough to be his own guardian, they took him in and loved him like the child they had always wanted. Miss Alva took up where his parents left off and babied him.

Chatty was unfazed by the Governor's remark, though, he was usually reined in by Cager. When he heard a certain tone to McCager Burnett's words, he straightened up and flew right.

This time, however, Chatty was aglow with the holiday spirit and nothing could spoil it. "Governor," he said, "once, my gardener was ill and the roses were in a very shabby way—as if they were Mona Windsor's wardrobe."

Mona was Atlanta society's premiere gossip. Though she had grown up in money and society, her father was an enormous gambler who lost vast sums. But Atlanta society was loyal, so if one were born at Piedmont Hospital, as was Mona, one was always part of that society. Even though her once-stately home was run down, even needing a new roof, she sponged, shamelessly, off the others who still had wealth and remained firmly rooted in the world of the upper crust. She earned her keep by spreading the kind of gossip that everyone loved to hear.

Crossing one arm over his massive chest, Chatty put his other hand to his chin, looking upward at the barn's rafters and thought for a moment. "I spent the better part of an hour sprucing up the roses to a suitable standard. It was terribly hot that day. I suffered so. It was close to 70 degrees."

The Governor shook his head with resignation. "Sometime, Chatty, remind me to introduce you to the real world."

Chatty put his hands on his hips and said, "Dear Governor, I was born to bring joy to those who have none. I am a purveyor of delight. Bountiful delight. Endless. Speaking of my notable talent for bringing happiness, I must tarry no longer, for I must cheer Fancy Sadie with these remarkably beautiful Christmas decorations."

"Chatham, do you think a horse in labor needs a decorated stall?" the Governor asked.

"Oh, yes, sir! Without question, I can make a marvelous difference in how she feels." He then turned his back and began sorting through the decorations, one-by-one, eventually pulling out four strands of battery-operated lights. He started to look for the batteries then decided to put the wreath up, first. It already had batteries!

In the stall, Stella and Bubba were carefully monitoring Fancy Sadie. A moment earlier, they'd bumped heads when Stella, talking soothingly to the Fancy Sadie, had turned suddenly while Bubba had his hand on the horse's side to see whether she was breathing rapidly.

"Excuse me!" Stella said at the same moment Bubba said, "I'm sorry." Then, something happened that neither expected. Their eyes locked. It was as if a magnet was drawing them together. Stella felt her heart beat rapidly. Everything around her melted away, completely disappearing. As her grandmother used to say, she felt "swimmy-headed." Growing up, she had always had a crush on Bubba, but she thought she'd dispensed with that girlish feeling long ago. Even at her lowest point of misery with Asher Bankwell, she had never thought of Bubba except when her mama mentioned something he had done on the farm.

Bubba, tall and lean, with startling blue eyes, moved toward her. They were in a magic bubble all on their own. And just as their lips were about to touch, she was startled out of the trance by Chatty's impatient voice. He could always be counted on to show up at the most imperfect time.

"Stella Faye!" he snapped impatiently. "Are you listening?"

Stella gathered herself before turning around and saying something hateful to him. She and Bubba looked sadly at each other and exchanged tight smiles.

She turned to Chatty and said, sarcastically. "Chatty, please forgive me for not always and forever giving you my undivided attention."

Chatty didn't recognize the sarcasm and, instead, smiled happily. He always loved it when Stella made him the center of her universe. "Sweet Stellie, that is quite alright. I feel certain you will do better in the future." Then, wagging a finger in her direction, "Let's just not allow it to happen again." He punctuated it with a smile. "I am in need, desperately, of something."

Stella reached into the pocket of her coat and pulled out a hair clip. She twisted her long, golden-red hair up and clipped it, which made startlingly evident her perfect, soft jawline and small nose that tipped upward ever so slightly. It was now Bubba's turn to feel "swimmy-headed." His first crush had been Lynn, then it became Stella. Then, long ago, Bubba had forced himself to forget about Stella by putting on a suit and tie and attending her wedding to Asher Bankwell. Of course, Bubba had just sat in his truck in the Peachtree Presbyterian church parking lot. This was as close as he would get. He just couldn't bring himself to go inside and witness that his feelings for Stella had to end.

"And you need what, Chatty?" she asked without a smile.

"Something to hang this wreath."

Stella motioned to her left where two sliding barn doors were pulled together. "Perhaps in that little storage room. Daddy always kept a toolbox in there. You should find a hammer and perhaps even some nails."

A wicked smile slid across Cager's face. "Do you even know what a hammer looks like?"

"Yes, thank you," Chatty said in a clipped tone.

But Cager wasn't letting go that easily. "Well, then, do you know how to you use one?"

"Apparently, it is not that challenging. I was over at my friend's house. Eloise Johnson. She has the most ignorant handy man. He's never heard of *Swan Lake*, the most beautiful ballet possible. If he can use a hammer, I most certainly can."

The Governor and Stella looked at each other while Bubba stared at Chatty, trying to figure out this creature. In just a moment, Chatty called out triumphantly, "Aha! I found one."

He came out of the closet, smiling broadly, so proud of himself, holding up his new-found treasure.

"Close," said McCager. "That's a ball peen hammer. You need a claw hammer."

Chatty turned the tool around, staring at it with a puzzled look. McCager walked over to the closet and there, right on top of the toolbox, was a claw hammer which he handed to Chatty.

"Oh my," he said. "It's so heavy."

"That's the point," the Governor said. "The weight drives the nail into the wood."

"This is turning out to be such an educational trip," Chatty said somewhat thoughtfully. The Governor dug around until he found a few nails the right size.

"Use this, it will hold the wreath."

Smiling, Chatty, eager to show how handy he was, went over to the stall to drive a nail into the door. Of course, within seconds, he was screaming in agony. "My thumb! My thumb!" McCager walked over and, grabbing the hammer from Chatty said, "It's like letting a child play with a butcher knife."

While the Governor was driving in the nail and Chatty was nursing his injured thumb, Bubba turned to Stella, "Sadie's too restless. She's up and down. Those aren't good signs."

"We can't lose this girl or her baby. I'd feel awful. I couldn't face Lynn and Ronnie." All the while, Big Black was watching everything very carefully.

With McCager having hung the wreath, Chatty now turned on the white lights and admired the gold ornaments and big red bow that adorned the greenery. It was, indeed, a stunning Christmas decoration. While admiring the expensive purchase he'd chosen, Chatty was also half-listening to Stella and Bubba's conversation. "Why don't y'all ask Pepper for help? He knows all about the birds and the bees," said Chatty. Straightening the wreath to perfection he added, "And birthing babies."

Stella looked up from stroking Fancy Sadie's neck and exclaimed, "Pepper?"

"Birthing babies?" Cager asked in a quizzical tone.

"Hm-huh." Chatty had returned to the church pew and was picking through the decorations.

"Chatham, explain yourself. What does Pepper and birthing babies have in common?" McCager Burnett was not fooling around.

Chatty was so focused on the decorations that he didn't look up. "Pepper brought a man and his wife to the house. She's howling in pain like a wolf during a full moon." Picking up a fancy, sizable sign that read *Merry Christmas*, he continued. "Miss Mama and Miss Alva are going to have to deliver her baby. Pepper explained it all to me."

It was, at that moment, on a Christmas Eve night, that quietness echoed through the Appalachian foothills. It became, truly, a silent night.

None of the other three could manage to speak.

Chapter Fourteen

Melissa was scared. And rightly so. Anyone in her place would have felt the same. Since she was five-years old, she'd had an awakening of sorts that she could plan her future as an adult—and she was firmly rooted in being a mother. She was resolute about it and proclaimed to all that she planned to have seven children, and that each child would have a name starting with the letter "C." She memorized the seven names so when she was older, she wrote them down in crayon. And, to this day, that piece of paper was tucked away with other special papers such as the marriage license between her and Daniel, her mother's chocolate cake recipe, and a newspaper clipping of her grandmother's obituary.

She'd had a baby doll with short, curly blonde hair named Cora Beth who Melissa toted everywhere. Every morning, she changed Cora Beth's nightgown for a pretty dress. When Cora Beth had a fever, Melissa would hold her and rock her while lovingly stroking her hair. She dabbed her face with cool water and always succeeded in nursing her back to health. Melissa made certain that Cora Beth was raised right, which, in the mountains, meant gathering in the church house, without fail, for Sunday school at Mt. Pisgah Baptist church, then every Sunday and Wednesday night. Together, Melissa and Cora Beth learned the Lord's prayer and sang joyfully in the choir. Cora Beth's favorite song was *I'll Fly Away*, but Melissa preferred *He'll Pilot Me.* Every night, they would say bedtime prayers, kneeling and repeating, "Now, I lay me down to sleep." Then they would name every person they wished to be protected and blessed, including the family dog, Sweet Tea.

Melissa's parents were amused by the reality that she gave to Cora Beth. But to Melissa, Cora Beth truly was real from the day Santa Claus left her under the Christmas tree—and she would have it no other way. When Melissa turned six and entered the first grade, Cora Beth was taken to school in the large, red brick building, built in 1936, where every grade, from first to twelfth, was housed. The third and fourth grade shared a room because one class had five students while the other class had six. Life in the Appalachians was much different than in Cleveland, which was, twenty-five miles away.

The teachers kindly accepted Cora Beth's attendance and went along with Melissa's fantasy. They even graded Cora Beth's papers, which usually had only her name, and excused her for the restroom when it was really Melissa who needed to go. As she prepared to enter the second grade, Melissa explained to Cora Beth that her education was complete and that Melissa's mother would now watch over her while Melissa went to school, alone. Though, eventually, Melissa accepted that Cora Beth wasn't real, she still kept the baby doll in her room and treated her with loving respect. Even now, after fifteen years of marriage, Melissa kept Cora Beth on a shelf in their bedroom closet. It reminded her of how long she'd prayed to have a baby. Painfully so. She and Daniel had almost given up hope when the doctor gave them the good news. At the time, Melissa thought she had a very bad virus because she'd been sick for days, surviving on saltine crackers and ginger ale.

They were elated. During the months that followed, Daniel often cooked supper and mopped the floor. He didn't want his wife to take any chance of losing the baby. For months, they planned for the day when they'd become parents. Daniel had built the most beautiful cradle. Now, ironically, she was about to deliver the baby by the light of a kerosene lamp, assisted by women with only rudimentary knowledge of the birthing process. The women were, however, sincere and determined to make Melissa comfortable. Daniel had assisted them in removing the stretchy black pants and oversized white sweater she'd been wearing, replacing them with a white cotton nightgown, trimmed in lace, that belonged to Martha Annie. It had been a Christmas gift two years ago, from Stella and, in fact, it was quite expensive. Her Mama loved it, but she had carefully hand washed and ironed it only once, then placed it in her cedar chest that set at the foot of her bed. She was saving it for a special occasion. And this was the most special occasion she could think of, though she knew that it might be ruined during giving birth. Martha Annie Jackson was completely selfless.

Miss Alva called Dr. Colby again who asked, among other things, about the timing of Melissa's contractions.

By this point, Melissa had almost grown used to the discomfort and rarely groaned loudly. The doctor instructed Miss Alva to have her breathe through her contractions and to continue gently encouraging her.

"If you can keep her calm, it will be much easier for her to have the baby. Sterilize a pair of scissors because you'll need to cut the umbilical cord. If you have some gauze handy, I'd like you to bandage the belly button afterwards. And don't forget what we talked about. You may have to give that baby a sharp smack on the butt to get his lungs working. When he, or she, cries, it'll be a beautiful sound because the baby'll no longer be depending on Melissa to breathe." "There's so much to take care of," Miss Alva noted.

"Don't you worry. Between yourself and Martha Annie, it'll all come naturally. Just keep the baby warm, wrapping it snug in a blanket, and place it on Melissa's chest so they can bond."

"What about Melissa?" Miss Alva inquired.

"Give her small sips of water while she's getting ready to deliver. But it sounds like she still has a little ways to go yet. You call me back in thirty minutes unless you need me sooner."

As Melissa waited for the next contraction, the thought of Cora Beth drifted into her mind. It helped to relax her. She remembered teaching Cora Beth to say the Lord's Prayer. Softly, she began repeating it, over and over. Then, singing it. As the others in the room heard her, peace seemed to blanket the room. Nerves were soothed and strength enveloped them.

ᘓ

The Governor held open the back door for Stella as they hurried in the house, having stomped the snow from their shoes on the porch. They heard voices and a cry of pain coming from down the hall.

"They must be in Mama's room," said Stella.

"Evenin' Spencer," the Governor said, then stopped and looked back. "Spencer, what are you doing here?"

"Master Colquitt required my services to assist with Christmas dinner."

Cager rolled his eyes. "Chatham never fails to surprise me." Still, he found himself chuckling as he followed Stella down the hall, using their flashlights. The sight of Spencer in his proper butler's attire, complete with bow tie, arranging sandwiches on a silver tray in an old-fashion kitchen, with a flickering kerosene lantern was an unimaginable sight.

"Well, that's something I'll hang onto for the rest of my days," he mumbled.

"Mama?" Stella asked through the crack between the door and its frame.

Soon, Martha Annie and Miss Alva both slipped out of the room and into the hall. As Miss Alva pulled the door closed behind them, they heard a painful wail come from inside the room.

"What the thunder is going on here?" McCager boomed as quietly as possible for him. Then, he fell into complete stunned silence as they explained the situation.

"Oh, my goodness!" Stella finally said after they absorbed the news. "Poor Melissa. From what I've heard, childbirth can be difficult enough... but in these conditions, it must be even more frightening."

"Well, one blessing is that her doctor is a friend of ours. George Colby," assured Miss Alva.

"Dang good doctor. He and the good Lord will see y'all through this," said Cager.

"We're starting to see trouble with Fancy Sadie in the barn."

"What's wrong?" asked Martha Annie.

"We don't know," Stella responded. "Her breathing and heart rate are up and she can't get comfortable. She lays down, then gets back up. She keeps doing the same thing over and over. Up and down." Stella paused, almost hating to ask lest it revealed anything about her feelings. "I heard that Pepper rescued Melissa?"

"Yes. He's such a sweet man," her Mama replied, smiling at her.

"Well, where is he now?" Stella asked.

Surprised by her question, both women looked at each other. "He wasn't in the kitchen?"

Cager chuckled. "Maybe he was, and I just didn't see him. When Stella and I hurried through the kitchen, I was so shocked to see Spencer, laying out triangle-shaped sandwiches on a silver tray, that I could've missed him completely."

"Here I am." And there he was. Handsome, sandy-haired Pepper with the perfect smile. When he and Stella had first met in the lobby of the King and Prince Hotel on St. Simons Island, they had laughed at the coincidence of his surname being Jackson while Stella's maiden name had been Jackson. Who would've guessed that, less than two years later, Pepper would be standing in the Jackson farmhouse amidst an event that he would remember, always. In his hands, he was holding a large black duffle bag.

"Mrs. Madison asked me to bring this with her when I got her out of the car." He handed it to Miss Alva. "There's probably something in here you might need. I just went out to the car to retrieve it."

"Oh, yes, thank you, dear Pepper," said Miss Alva, who then looked at Martha Annie. "I'm willing to bet there aren't any diapers in here since the hospital usually supplies those."

"When Stella and Lynn were born, we still used cloth diapers. Speaking of which, I can make a few diapers from a couple of Sims' old tee shirts. And I have plenty of safety pins in my sewing cabinet."

Stella looked deeply at her Mama and processed that sentence. Sims Jackson had been dead for many years. She opened her mouth to ask but thought twice about it and decided not to. If her daddy's tee shirts meant that much to her Mama, to keep for so many years, she would not draw attention to it.

"That's a good ole mountain girl for you," the Governor said, with approval ringing in his voice. "I have no doubt, no doubt at all that you two will pull this off like champions."

"Excuse me." The intonation of Spencer's British voice filled the small hall. "I have prepared a tray of sandwiches. Shall I serve?"

Suddenly, they all realized that no one had eaten since morning. Pepper, eager to arrive at the farm and, as only his heart knew, to see Stella, had only grabbed a cup of coffee as he was leaving his hotel.

"We should get back to the barn and see if Bubba needs help, but we have a few minutes to eat something, quickly," Cager said. "Thank you, Spencer. I now applaud Mr. Colquitt's foresight in bringing you along." Cager's characteristic chuckle followed that remark.

"Martha Annie, you eat first and I'll stay with Melissa. Then, we'll swap out and I'll eat," said Miss Alva.

In the dim light of the flashlight the Governor had been holding, along with the light from Pepper's flashlight which he kept in the SUV, Stella and Pepper had barely been able see each other. And still, there was an undeniable warmth that passed between them. The truth was that Stella, who had looked forward to having Pepper join them for Christmas, now nearly regretted it. She was rediscovering feelings for Bubba, a crush she'd had in her younger days, once felt so deeply. Their "near kiss" had been interrupted, predictably, by Chatty who was often the scene stealer. In all her years of high school, she had prayed nightly that Bubba, the dazzling team quarterback, would notice her one day. When the cheerleaders divided up the football players between them, to make signs to encourage them, posting them on the walls in the school, she always made sure she got Bubba's name. Kelly McGee, who also had a crush on Bubba, protested, leaving the rest of the cheerleaders to vote who should get Bubba. Stella, the most popular girl in school, always won.

Now, standing here in the hall, Stella knew she had to put on her game face for Pepper.

"You made it. I'm so glad," she said sweetly. He was in between her and McCager, so she put her arm around his waist and gave him a sideways hug—something any decent Southern woman would've done to a good friend. "Will you join us for sandwiches?"

Pepper was no fool. He was a highly trained marshal and man with a lot of intuition. He sensed a shift in Stella's feelings from when he last saw her, three days earlier.

"First, I need to bring in more firewood to keep the fire going and the water boiling. Where's the wood stack?"

"Water boiling?" she asked.

"One of Dr. Colby's instructions," Martha Annie said, then told Pepper there was wood piled on the back porch as well as a stack on the front porch. Another cry of pain came from in the bedroom and the group broke up, instantly. Pepper went for firewood, Miss Alva back to Melissa who was clutching Daniel's hand, while the others followed Spencer to the kitchen.

Pepper, hurt spreading over his heart, tried to appear upbeat. "Where's Chatty?"

"In the barn," Stella replied as she picked up one of Chatty's fine china plates. Then, reaching for a sandwich, she was stopped by Spencer who said, "Madam Stella, please allow me the pleasure of serving you." He pulled out a chair for Stella as well as one for Martha Annie.

"The barn!" Pepper exclaimed.

"Don't ask," McCager said, pulling out his own chair and sitting down. "Some things are better seen than explained. Join us out there, later, and you'll see for yourself."

"That Chatty. He's always full of surprises." Pepper tried to be lighthearted as he headed out the door. But Stella, who knew him best, heard the real emotion in his voice.

Unfortunately, she had not fooled him. Not one tiny bit.

Chapter Fifteen

On the porch, Pepper found a full stack of firewood, the top row covered in a slight layer of snow, having been protected by the house's overhang. Using a lantern, he then made his way to the front porch where there was another stack of logs, at least two days' worth. As a marshal, he was trained to look past the present and into the possible future.

Wisely, he decided to bring firewood from the back porch and scatter it on the front so it could dry completely should they need it. As he worked, he thought, perhaps too much, about Stella. A chance meeting on St. Simons had introduced him to one of the most beautiful, kindest women he had ever known. To top that, they had teamed together to bring down an intricate money laundering scheme that included her now ex-husband, Asher Bankwell. Stella had introduced him to the Burnetts and Chatham Colquitt which is how and why they wound up on Sapelo Island, solving a murder mystery that had entangled an innocent young man, the nephew of the Burnetts' longtime housekeeper.

Pepper was infatuated. He had been so committed to his job for so long that he rarely thought about romance though he had dated many women. What Pepper had not realized was that, while many women had been taken by his charm and good looks and were wishful for a long-term relationship and, hopefully, marriage—he never cared.

Until he met Stella.

Perhaps, he thought to himself as he carried an arm load of wood to the front porch, it was true what people say, that you always want the one who doesn't want you. But it had seemed to him that he and Stella were growing closer. Twice, they had almost kissed. And when the Burnetts invited him to spend Christmas here with them, they had dangled the carrot that Stella's family farm was right next to theirs.

"Maybe this was a mistake, coming here to these mountains," he muttered to himself as he spread the wood across the front porch to dry. He then considered that maybe he was overreacting, one way or the other. Either she was playing hard to get or she was distracted by all that was happening. Firmly, he decided to let go of the worry and see what happened.

ᘓ

Inside, at the kitchen table, Stella, her mama, and the Governor enjoyed being served by Spencer so they could rest a few minutes while each talked of the events that had unfolded over the past few hours.

"Spencer, this potato salad is excellent," Stella said. "The best I've ever tasted. Thank you."

"Your compliment is most appreciated." He bowed slightly. "Most fortunately, I was able to complete the salad before the loss of electricity."

The Governor patted his stomach. He had a small ulcer, and it was bothering him. He always pretended to be confident and in charge. He fooled everyone except Miss Alva, who knew that the tough, former Marine was affected by stress as much as anyone. Lately, he had been working on a complicated estate case where every family member of the deceased client refused to work together or be appeased.

"Is it possible to get a glass of sweet milk?" he asked, using the mountain term that distinguished regular milk from buttermilk. "Or buttermilk."

Martha Annie stood up and said, "Which would you rather have? I have both."

"Buttermilk, please."

Stella finished up her third small sandwich and potato salad then settled back comfortably in her chair. Wrapping her arms around herself and sighing contently, she eyed the old KitchenAid mixer that her mama had been using as long back as she could remember. Nothing about this old kitchen had changed in many years. There was nothing fancy or even modern about it except for the range Stella had bought her for Christmas a few years ago when her other one, almost forty years old, had quit working and parts were no longer available. This kitchen held so many memories for her. It's where she and Lynn had spent just about every summer, helping their Mama can vegetables from their garden. She looked at the original cabinets that Martha Annie had attempted to spruce up with a coat of pale green paint. Stella smiled, remembering all the times she had to scrub them down after they'd put up corn for freezing. It was such a messy job, the cream from the cobs flying all over the kitchen as they scraped them. She chuckled to herself, recalling the time she had to stand on the countertop, with a broom, trying to get kernels of corn off the ceiling. This was home, and nothing would ever compare. She felt loved and protected here, like no other place she knew. She shivered with the perfect feeling of comfort. She felt that in the barn with Bubba. She realized that she had gotten "above her raisin'" but she had rediscovered the solid ground of her upbringing.

Her mama's words interrupted her thoughts. "I'm goin' to relieve Alva. Stella, maybe you'd better go check on Fancy Sadie. And take Bubba and Chatty something to eat."

Spencer spoke up. "I shall put together two supper plates. Which should I use?"

Martha Annie pulled out a heavy paper plate and clear wrap. She gave a small laugh when she saw the look of disdain on Spencer's face. "I get the message. I have a couple of pottery dishes. You can use those, instead." That task complete, Miss Mama headed to the bedroom from where an occasional cry of pain could be heard.

Before Miss Alva came into the kitchen, the Governor took a swig of buttermilk, set down the glass, and commanded to Stella, "Now, tell me how it feels to come home? I see such a comfort covering you from head to toe. You're very different from the citified Stella I've seen in the past dozen years."

She smiled slightly. "Governor, I'm a country mouse. Plain and simple."

ɷ

When Stella opened the barn door, she saw a delightfully happy scene. Chatty had worked his magic on Fancy Sadie's stall. Festive lights, with batteries, covered her stall and strung around the stall door. Even the window where Big Black was keeping his watch was lined with lights. Chatty was just finishing up the lights around Big Black's stall and his side of the window. Chatty had even hung the wreath on Sadie's door and the *Merry Christmas!* sign on Scout's stall door.

Stella clapped and called out, "Bravo! It looks wonderful! Plus, it gives us more light, which we need."

Chatty smiled proudly. He loved for Stella to brag on him. "It looks more than just wonderful," he replied. "It looks bodacious. Yes, that's what it is. Bodacious."

"You're right. It *is* bodacious!" They laughed merrily together

"Oh, Stella, I want to entertain this world with such beauty." He always delighted Stella in moments like this because his was such a child-like spirit. It had occurred to Stella that it was because he got very little attention from his mother. She was glamorous, and "breathtakingly gorgeous" was how Chatty described her.

Bubba was not as cheerful. Concern covered his face as he slid open Fancy Sadie's stall door and he stepped out, walking to Stella who was still caught up in Chatty's excitement.

"Spencer fixed you and Chatty a plate. Mama wanted to give y'all paper plates, but it horrified him."

"You brought me buttermilk?"

She smiled and nodded. "I remember how much you always loved buttermilk. Mama had it out for McCager who, get this, admitted he has a small ulcer. He's forever acting like nothing fazes him. Anyway, while she had the jug out, I poured a glass for you." Bubba smiled weakly, causing Stella to ask, "What is it?"

Indicating Fancy Sadie with his hand, he said, "Something is wrong. Really wrong."

Stella crossed to the stall and knelt down, beside Fancy Sadie, when, all a-sudden, the horse rose up, startling Stella who had to quickly jump back.

"You okay in there?" Bubba called.

"I'm fine. But you're right. Something's really wrong."

Stella walked over and sat down with Bubba on a hay bale while he removed the plastic sheet covering his plate, hungrily eating his first sandwich. As he started on his second, he asked, "Why are these sandwiches so small?"

Before she could answer, Chatty arrived to explain, in his lilting Southern accent, "That is the proper way to prepare a sandwich. Babe Paley always served petite sandwiches and vegetables. Everything was small. And, because it was Babe, all of society began serving petite sandwich, tiny carrots, green beans, potatoes."

Bubba looked at Chatty as though he was trying to teach him algebra. He had no idea who Babe Paley was and less of an idea why anyone would eat tiny vegetables.

"Chatty, here's all I can say to that—people who're eating tiny vegetables ain't workin' a farm, because we eat hardy."

"Chatty, are you hungry?" Stella asked.

"Not yet, thank you. And of this discussion, I can take no more," Chatty proclaimed then sashayed over to where he again started to dig through his decorations.

"So, what do you think's wrong with Sadie?"

Shaking his head while watching Fancy Sadie in her stall, "She's just not as calm as she should be. And what really worries me is how worried that Big Black is, pacin' the stall and lookin' in on her from time to time. Animals are intuitive. You know, Stella, you can look in their eyes and see the truth of how they feel. Sadie's eyes are filled with pain."

Stella nodded, thinking about it while Chatty pranced with joyful jolly over to Big Black's stall with silver bells clanging together as he sang *Silver Bells*. Resourcefully, he hung them from the stall by putting them around a sturdy, black iron post on the stall door. He clapped his hands together, placing them under his chin, closed his eyes, smiled sweetly and said, "Dorothy Draper could have done no better."

Bubba was lost in Chatty's world, a place he could not understand. He stared at him a moment, then finally shook his head and dove into the potato salad, shoveling a large amount into his mouth.

"This salad is delicious. Did your mama make it?" he asked.

"Chatty's butler, Spencer. It must be a recipe he brought from London." While Bubba finished eating, Stella watched Fancy Sadie. It was obvious she was growing more and more uncomfortable. She was up and down and pacing the stall while nickering in pain.

"Bub, you don't reckon' the foal's breech, do you?"

He looked at Stella. "That's what I'm afraid of. I just didn't want to say it out loud. If it is, the good Lord will have to help us 'cuz without a vet here, we could lose both of them."

It felt so natural when she slipped her arm through Bubba's and laid her head on his shoulder. Bubba laid his head against hers and put one of his hands over hers. For a couple of minutes, no one said a word. Stella was so comfortable in a barn, wearing a pair of Wellies and being with Bubba. Chatty paid them utterly no attention because he was lost in a world of his own. He found some twine and strung red and gold globes on it and said under his breath, "Chatham, you are brilliant to have thought to bring twine." He went on decorating and making himself happy, believing he was making others happy.

It didn't matter anyway since Stella and Bubba were lost in a world of *their* own. After a moment, Bubba turned, and slowly lifted her chin. He looked deeply into Stella's green eyes. Yes, his feelings for her, the ones he so desperately tried to forget ever since the day she got married, they were still there, stronger even. And then, he kissed her, softly. Stella felt herself melt, a warm glow spreading over her. She scooted closer and laid her head back on his shoulder and pulled her arm tighter through his. There they were, happily together—until the spell was broken by McCager Burnett's booming voice.

"In all my born life, I've never seen a barn decorated like this!" Knowing how much Chatham loved to be bragged on, he continued, "Chatty, a job well-done."

Stella and Bubba quickly straightened up before the Governor saw them through the dim light. But someone else had seen them.

Pepper Culpepper's heart had just been broken. Perhaps for the first time ever.

Chapter Sixteen

Stella, suddenly seeing Pepper but ignoring the now-awkward situation, jumped up and walked over to the Governor, asking, "How're things going up at the house?"

"Alva came in the kitchen to get something to eat while I was having coffee." He chuckled before continuing. "Incidental to this story is that Spencer was appalled at having to make me a cup of *instant* coffee, using water boiling in the fireplace."

Stella nodded and smiled. "It's quite an education for him and Chatty. But I think they're enjoying themselves."

"It'll do 'em good. But back to your question. Alva phoned the doctor and asked when he last examined Melissa. He said it was just two days ago, and he did a scan. The baby's situated perfectly. That helped Alva's feelings a great deal. Her labor pains are three minutes apart and he told Alva that when they're a minute apart Melissa needed to begin pushing. When I left the house, she was carrying on something awful. I think her fear has elevated the pain in her mind."

Meanwhile, since no one else had offered, and because he was more than curious, Pepper decided to introduce himself to Bubba. He also thought that, somehow, this would help ease his discomfort of the moment. Bubba had gone off to the fourth stall to get some sweet feed for Big Black. Both the stallion and the laboring mare had plenty of hay in their stalls. And so, Pepper decided to wait near Fancy Sadie's stall for him to return, admiring Chatty's decorations, out loud.

"Chatty, you made the barn so cheerful especially with the power out. It reminds me of all that is Christmas."

Chatty smiled widely. "I believe in being prepared so I bought battery-powered lights."

"Brillant," Pepper replied.

The truth of the matter was that Spencer had accompanied Chatty to Phipps Plaza. He also drove Chatty, who had a driver's license but refused to drive himself. In years past, he'd had a full-time driver, but Chatty didn't use him much. McCager, who had a yearly accounting of Chatty's expenditures, saw the driver's salary as a needless expense and suggested Chatty pay Spencer a quarter of what the driver was paid and save the rest. Chatty wasn't easy to convince.

"It will harm my image. Everyone knows how rich I am. There will be unpleasant gossip about that." He shuddered.

"Tell them you've decided to save the money and will be giving it to charity." He paused and looked

Chatty square in the eye. "Then, do it." Spencer happily accepted the raise in salary and drove while Chatty sat in the back seat. Always in the back seat. For image purposes.

So, it was Spencer, with him at the upscale shopping mall, who suggested the battery-powered lights. At that point, neither Spencer nor Chatty could have imagined that Chatty would be using them to decorate a stall for a mare who was about to foal. They were going a long way out of the city and Spencer, not knowing how many outlets they would find, thought it a good idea. But it was just like Chatty to take the credit. The way he looked at it was that he employed Spencer, so he owned creative rights to any of his ideas.

In the barn, Chatty began pointing out various decorations. "Did you notice the Merry Christmas sign I hung over there for Scout? And be sure to see Big Black's stall. It's very becoming for an important stallion and father-to-be."

As he was bragging on himself, Bubba returned with a half-filled bucket of sweet feed. Though he didn't show it outwardly, his heart was soaring over the kiss with Stella. To the Governor and Stella, he called, "There's more sweet feed missin'. I've been here for hours and I ain't heard nothin'. Raccoons make a noise."

"Probably a possum then," the Governor said.

Bubba shook his head. "Too high up for a possum." He shrugged and took the bucket into Big Black's stall and poured it into his feed trough.

As he came out of the stall, Pepper was waiting. "We haven't met. I'm Jackson Culpepper. I'm staying with the Burnetts for a couple of days."

Bubba, who had never heard him mentioned in any way when it came to Stella, offered his hand and they shook, hard. "Nice to meet'cha. Bubba McCoy. Are you the marshal who rescued Melissa?"

"I am, yep."

"You did a mighty good deed. Mighty good."

Situations like that were part of Pepper's training so he was a bit uncomfortable with praise. "I'm just glad we came along when we did. How's Fancy Sadie doing?"

Before he could answer, Stella joined the men, worried about them talking together, alone. "So, you two've met?"

Pepper gave her a rather icy look, a look she had never seen before so the expression was not lost on her. She withered a bit and knew he was putting her in her place.

"I introduced myself." Stella felt the chill sweep over her body.

"Please, forgive me. I've been so caught up between the two babies bein' born that I didn't realize."

"I'm plum happy to meet the man who rescued Melissa," Bubba replied cheerfully. He was soaring so he was more cheerful and talkative than normal. It had taken twenty-five years to get that kiss. He was ten years old when he started falling in love with Stella.

After sufficiently bragging on Chatty, McCager walked over to the group, unaware he was about to save the day for Stella by interrupting.

"Bubba, how's Sadie doin'?"

"I'm worried somethin' is wrong with the foal."

"Like what?"

"Maybe breeched."

The Governor knew that was a serious situation. "Do you really think that?"

"Sadie's unusually uncomfortable. She's up and down and twisting like she has colic. I've only helped birth a horse a couple of times. Once was helpin' Ronnie and Lynn but the vet was there. He said, 'Horses are big babies. They take lots of attention.' Now, calfing I know about. And cows are sturdy." He shrugged. "Maybe I'm overthinkin'."

McCager Burnett shook his head. "No, Bubba, I don't believe you're overthinking. One of us needs to go in and check the position of the foal."

By this time, Chatty had insinuated himself into the gathering. "Go in? Go in? What could that possibly mean?"

This was too delicious. The Governor would enjoy, beyond measure, the explanation. "Either Bubba or I need to go inside the horse and see what position the foal's in. Normally, the front feet come out first, followed by the head."

"Oh," is all Chatty said. At first.

Then, after just another moment, his eyes grew big, and he grabbed his stomach as though he were about to throw up. "Goodness gracious, Lord have mercy. I am in the middle of primitives. Pure savages."

"Oh, Chatty, stop it," Stella said a bit sharply, rolling her eyes. "This is part of nature. You arrived just the same way, for heaven's sake."

"Do *not* compare me to a horse. I had a fine birth at Piedmont hospital attended by society's most prestigious doctor."

"Are you sure, Chatty?" Pepper asked with a mischievous smile. "Or did the stork bring you?"

Everyone laughed and his face reddened. "I believe I should go on to the house."

"Go ahead," Stella waved her hand toward the door. "But what's going on up there is more traumatizing than what's going on down here."

A mixture of worry and fear covered Chatty's face. "I knew I should've stayed in Buckhead or Sea Island."

The Governor, ignoring Chatty's upset, asked Bubba, "You want to, or shall I?"

"I will," Bubba replied. "I think there're surgical gloves in the closet only 'cause the vet left them here a few months ago when he put his hand in one of the cow's mouths. Somethin' was stuck in her throat."

"Oh, my word!" Chatty protested loudly which made Bubba laugh while the others suppressed their amusement.

"I can go in barehanded if need be. I've done that plenty of times."

A shudder of disgust shook Chatty, still attired in khaki pants, stuck inside Sims' old boots, and the sock cap. The Governor saw this and pulled out his strongest tone of command.

"Chatham, I think it'd do you plenty good to stay and watch. You need a glimpse into the real world."

"I don't like the real world," Chatty said casually in childlike innocence. "I like *my* world. In my world, I'd send Spencer out to watch for me." Chatty saw the look of aggravation on the Governor's face and it hit him deeply. The Burnetts were the only parents he had now, so his desire to please the Governor was greater than his fear and disgust.

In a small voice, Chatty relented, "Okay, I'll stay. I'll just go over here and sit on this bale of hay."

And just as he sat down, Bubba emerged from the closet, where Chatty had gotten the hammer and nails, pulling on blue latex gloves as he walked past.

"Chatham," said the Governor. "Come and watch this."

"I'm fine right here, Sir."

"Chatham." It was McCager Burnett's sternest voice. Chatty braced himself, then got up and dragged himself across the floor to stand by the Governor. Stella and Pepper were both completely unaffected by the sight of what was about to happen. Stella was a farm girl. Pepper, as a Marshal, had worked many bloody cases. It was hard to upset either.

"Stella, will you stay beside Sadie and keep her calm?" Bubba asked. Wordlessly, Stella stepped inside the stall and began loving Sadie, talking soothingly to her. Bubba moved her tail out of the way and lifted a gloved hand.

That's the last thing Chatty remembered before he slumped gently to the floor, landing at the Governor's feet.

ଊ

Miss Alva was timing Melissa's contractions with her wristwatch. She knew she was one of only a few friends who still wore a watch, but McCager had given her the small Rolex years ago and she prized it greatly. He had been so loving to buy it for her. It was his first major purchase when life became more comfortable for them.

"We're at two minutes. I'll get Dr. Colby on the phone." While Martha Annie was keeping warm washcloths on Melissa's forehead, Miss Alva picked up the phone to dial, then thought twice and replaced the phone on the hook. She reached over and took Melissa's hand.

"Darlin' girl, this will soon be over. Just a little while longer. When the contractions start coming one minute apart, you'll need to push with all your might." Melissa nodded, trying to be brave, while Daniel held her hand. "We can be confident the Lord will guide and provide."

Martha Annie smiled at her old friend. She was proud of her. It had crossed her mind that all of this might not be so easy for Alva. She'd wanted children, all her life, with all her heart. Now, she was selflessly helping another woman bring a child into the world. Having reassured Melissa, she dialed Dr. Colby. He answered the moment it rang.

"Are we there yet?" he asked calmly.

"Just about," Alva replied. She looked at her watch and timed the next contraction. "She's at one and a half minutes between contractions."

"After the next one, let's have Melissa start pushing."

Miss Alva relayed the message then, watching her, timed her pains. Calmly, she said, "With the next one, push down, hard." Martha Annie folded the blankets to the foot of the bed and gently put down a towel. She had another towel waiting to wrap the baby so they could clean it up before handing it to Melissa. Earlier, Miss Alva had asked if they knew whether the baby was a boy or a girl.

"We wanted to be surprised," Daniel said. "Besides, all that matters is that the baby's healthy."

In the kitchen, Spencer, with nothing to do, was sitting at the kitchen table, sipping hot tea and nibbling on a sandwich. He heard the first tortured grunt when Melissa began to push. Like Master Colquitt, he was in uncharted waters.

But, unlike Master Colquitt, he did not faint.

Chapter Seventeen

McCager Burnett had no sympathy. Not one shred. He was a crusty, old Marine who had been conditioned to the worst situations any man could imagine. That is to say that Chatty's fainting at the prospect of seeing something did not sit well with him.

He picked up a nearby bucket, marched outside, then returned with it filled with snow and dumped it on Chatty's head. Instantly, Chatty came to and sat up, shaking his head fiercely and wiping the snow from his face. Stella, of course, felt sorry for her friend and hurried over, kneeling beside Chatty, helping him.

Chatty was bewildered. "What happened?"

Stella pointed to McCager. "The Governor is what happened. After you fainted."

"*I fainted?*" Chatty often talked in italics. "Stella, I've never fainted in my life. Why would I faint now? And what is this snow about?"

"You fainted when Bubba started checking the position of Fancy Sadie's foal. The snow was meant to help bring you around."

Chatty was embarrassed and quickly thought of an explanation. "Oh, my. I've had a terrible ear infection.

It obviously affected my balance. That must've been what happened."

"Of course," Stella said sweetly, glancing up to see the Governor shake his head and roll his eyes.

The Governor was no longer concerned with Chatty. He walked back, over to the stall, where Pepper was watching Bubba. Stella helped Chatty to his feet and whispered, "Please, come over here with me and watch Bubba. The Governor's upset. You can do this. I know you can."

Chatty would do anything to please Stella. It was as though she could cast some sort of spell over him. Chatty adjusted his sock cap, making certain the pom-pom at the end of it wasn't wet but still fluffy. With Stella holding his hand, he bravely joined the Governor and Pepper. The Governor cut Chatty a sideward glance and said in a stern voice, "Don't stand here if you're only going to faint again."

"I feel terrible about that, Governor. I've never fainted. I suppose it was all the excitement. Along with the ear infection, of course. It all just threw me off-balance," Chatty said lightly and nonchalantly.

"I see," the Governor replied. "Just want to warn you, it only gets worse from here."

Chatty, white as a sheet, nodded, "Yes, sir. I understand." Then, suddenly, Chatty felt warm air in his ear. It was Big Black sticking his head out the stall door, rubbing his nose against Chatty's ear. Chatty jumped back until he realized what was happening.

Stella laughed merrily. "Chatty, it's just like that feral cow on Sapelo Island. The one who had a crush on you and broke into your bedroom that night."

"She was attracted by the sandalwood in my custom-created cologne that I have made in Paris," Chatty said, indignant, returning to his usual self. Big Black was obviously taken with Chatty, though. He seemed to have forgotten about his child, soon to be born.

"This time," Stella said. "I think it's all you."

Chatty was somewhat pleased. Big Black was soothing Chatty's bruised feelings. Plus, Chatty could stand there and pet Big Black without having to watch the unsightly action happening in the next stall.

The Governor turned his attention away from Chatty and toward Pepper. With his arms folded across his chest and watching Bubba, he asked, "Do you ride?"

"I grew up within the Memphis city limits but my uncle had a farm in Olive Branch, Mississippi, just over the state line. He had horses so I started riding when I was young. Sometimes, the good folks at Sea Island allow me to come out there and ride."

"Nice to hear. We might need your expertise in the next little while."

"I helped a marshal on a case in Wyoming, once. An escaped fugitive. We had to ride on horseback, up into the mountains."

"You catch him?"

"Actually, it was a woman. And, no, not those two days on horseback. But when we rode into the nearest town, we tracked her to a beauty salon. We traipsed right in, during the middle of her shampoo, and arrested her." Pepper chuckled at the memory.

The Governor found a chuckle in it, too. Bubba was still checking Sadie, so no one said a word to him until he pulled out his hand and arm. He breathed a heavy sigh and walked over to McCager who was standing between Pepper and Stella. Cager was completely blind to the kiss Pepper had seen when they first walked into the barn. However, he sensed that something was going on. Normally, Stella would be hanging by Pepper, yet the two had barely spoken since coming into the barn. And Stella had kept her distance. Bubba pulled off the messy glove, turning it inside out, then wadding it into a ball.

"Good news and bad news."

"I always enjoy hearin' the bad news, first," the Governor said with a tinge of sarcasm in his voice.

Tossing the glove in the trash bin, Bubba said, "For sure, there's a problem." The air went out of Stella, and she slumped her shoulders. McCager and Pepper were undaunted and Chatty was caught up in the love that his new friend was giving him.

"The good news is that it's not as bad as it could be."

"What's wrong?"

"It feels to me like that the foal has a foot curled under which we *should* be able to reposition. The foal can't come out till that's fixed. Care to give us, second opinion?" he said to McCager who was undeterred by very little, if anything.

"Most certainly. It's been a while since I've gotten to be a farmer." Bubba slid the door open and stepped out of the stall while McCager stepped in. As he walked to the closet to get a set of gloves, he passed Stella, squeezing her arm. She smiled affectionately and winked. It was that this time, Chatty, who was facing them, saw what happened but waited until Bubba passed.

"Governor, I'm going to step out to get some fresh air. I'll be right back," Stella said, exiting the barn with Chatty right on her heels.

Outside, Stella breathed in the cold, crisp winter air. The snow had stopped, and the sky was now clear and she looked up at the magnificent, starry heavens above.

"Stella!" Chatty whispered loudly. A bit dreamy eyed, Stella turned toward around to face him. It was written all over her face. Still, he had to ask in order to make sure that she knew he was alert and aware, completely recovered from his "fainting."

"What was that about?"

"What was what about?" she asked, innocently.

Chatty threw his head toward the barn. "Bubba."

Inside the barn, Pepper couldn't pretend either that he hadn't seen the affections exchanged between Stella and the man who'd just walked past him, joining McCager in the stall.

For the first time since meeting Stella Bankwell, US Marshal Culpepper felt like the odd man out.

☙

With every contraction, Melissa pushed. Since Miss Alva had never had a baby, she was expecting it to arrive within fifteen minutes of active labor. She and Dr. Colby had agreed to stay on the phone until the baby arrived. Martha Annie had sterilized a pair of scissors and, holding a tiny spot on the handles, dropped them into a plastic bag, ready to cut the umbilical cord. But, first, they needed a baby. Daniel, Martha Annie, and Miss Alva were all warm, kind and encouraging. And while Melissa was still scared, the pains were now so intense that she was getting to the point where she thought only of the pain and not of her fear.

"How long should we expect this stage to last," Miss Alva asked Dr. Colby.

"Alva, there are times I've seen it last as long as three hours." Being married to a politician, she had, long ago, grown used to hiding her emotions in public. But this was such stunning news, that she blanched and her face went blank. Daniel was completely involved with Melissa, trying both to calm and to coach her. But he had heard the question.

"Miss Alva, what did the doctor say? How long?" He looked at her expectantly.

She held up her finger, pretending she was still listening to Dr. Colby. She didn't know what to say. It turned out that she was an undiscovered actress because she would nod from time to time as though she was still listening. She focused her attention on the lovely lace curtain that covered the window behind Martha Annie and the blue, yellow, and white floral curtains that were pushed back but which could be drawn together for more privacy. Martha Annie's bedroom was cozy and comfortable, though nothing fancy.

The furniture was decades old, bought when Martha Annie and Sims first married. Since Martha Annie was a little girl, she had saved money for the time when she would marry. She had a hope chest—an old trunk her great-uncle had given her—that she filled with needlepointed squares she could make into pillows, and anything else that might come her way. When her great-grandmother died, she had a brand new set of kitchen towels with the sales tag still attached. As they were cleaning out her house, Martha Annie's mother found the towels and asked her sister if she might have them for Martha Annie's hope chest. She was so proud to receive those towels and, though they were now old and looking worn, they were precious to her. By the time she was fourteen, Martha Annie was well known for her sewing skills, so she took in alterations and once even made a dress for a woman at their church, earning seven dollars. When Sims asked her to marry him, he had no idea she had any savings at all.

"Like most mountain people, I'm a poor, 'umble man. But I'll work hard to make us a good place to live, and you won't find a man to love you more than I do."

Sims Jackson was known as the best-looking man in those parts and Martha Annie's pretty looks matched his. So, one day, they married in a small church wedding. The bride wore a dress she'd sewn herself. Then she and her new husband went over the mountain to Cherokee, North Carolina, for their honeymoon. At first, they lived in a tiny little house Sims' daddy owned until Sims' grandfather died, three years later, and left to Sims what was known as "the old homeplace." No one argued against that because Sims had helped his grandfather on the farm since he'd been eight years old. As the years went by, Sims worked hard and bought more acreage whenever possible until he had a sizable piece of farm land.

But it was Martha Annie who had produced the biggest surprise when they'd returned from their honeymoon. Their little house had an old, iron post bed, ancient sofa, and a rocking chair that was a castoff. It was tattered and battered.

One morning, while they were standing at the kitchen counter eating breakfast, since they didn't yet have a kitchen table, Martha Annie asked, "Sims, would you be of a mind to let me buy us some furniture?

Sims had just taken a bite of scrambled eggs. He hastily swallowed, then set his fork on the plate and said, "Sweetheart, I told you when I asked you to be my wife that I ain't got no money. I make enough from granddaddy to pay the bills and to feed us but there's nothin' extra. I do plan on buildin' us a kitchen table one day," he joked, "Otherwise, we just have to make do, I'm afraid."

"I have money," she said softly.

He smiled, not expecting it to be much. "You do?" He tried to say it in a cheerful and not a mocking way. "How much have you got?" he asked as he picked up his cup and took a sip of coffee.

"Four hundred dollars." Martha Annie said it flatly, with a matter-of-fact tone.

Sims Jackson nearly choked on his coffee. "Four hundred dollars?! How'cha get that much?" He was stunned.

"I've been savin' since I was fourteen. You know how I took in sewin' and sold eggs to Mr. Mincey at the store. And when Miss McGee was so sick, her daughter up in Asheville, who married a wealthy man, paid me eight dollars a week to check on her every day, fix her somethin' to eat and clean the house."

Sims shook his head in disbelief. "My beautiful Martha Annie, that's yourn money and you do with it whatever pleases you."

So, she went into town, to Gordon Furniture, and bought a new sofa with a chair to match as well as a complete bedroom suite that included a double bed with headboard and footboard, a mattress and box-spring, a chifforobe, and a vanity with an enormous round mirror and two drawers on each side. She even bought a kitchen table with four chairs and still had seventy-six dollars left over which she put in an old coffee can and hid it behind their groceries. Over the years, when she had an extra dollar or two, she put that in the can, too. All of the furniture, she still used today—though she had bought a new mattress a few years ago.

It was in that bed where Melissa Madison was struggling to bring her baby into the world. Miss Alva had put Daniel off long enough. She finally placed her hand over the phone and said, "It could be any time or it might take a while longer."

"It's done been an hour," he said.

"She has to keep pushing until the baby's in birthing position." Daniel nodded and returned his full attention to Melissa.

To Dr. Colby, she said, "I need to step away for a quick break. Is there anything else? If not, I'll lay the receiver on the table, but please stay on the line until I get back." She listened to what George Colby was saying.

Calmly, she said, "That's wonderful. Thank you, Dr. Colby."

To Daniel, she said, "I just need to visit the powder room." When Miss Alva got to the door, she looked back and caught Martha Annie's eye. With a slight tilt of her head, she motioned for her to follow.

Martha Annie stood up. "Daniel, I'm goin' to warm this washcloth." Before leaving, she raised the wick higher on the kerosene lamp by the bedside, for more light, and picked up the small flashlight. When the two women were halfway down the hall, Miss Alva took Martha Annie by arm and guided her into the bathroom.

"George Colby just told me that this phase of labor could last hours."

"Oh, my. That wasn't the experience I had givin' birth. One or more of us could have a nervous breakdown before then," Martha Annie said trying to lighten the mood, adjusting her flashlight so they could see each other's faces.

"That's not all. He said that if she hasn't had this baby in three or so hours, then her body may not be ready. He may even need to perform a C-section." Miss Alva, always a lady, was speaking in gentle language. But Martha Annie, who'd had two babies, understood well.

"Since we're not in a hospital where the doctor could rush her into surgery, we might lose both Melissa and the baby." Martha Annie's words were grave.

The two women stood in the beam of the small flashlight looking at one other with fear and concern.

Their blood, Martha Annie thought, would be on our hands.

Chapter Eighteen

McCager Burnett, the mountain man, not the well-dressed, polished attorney and former Governor of the state of Georgia, was examining the foal still "stuck" in his mother's womb.

Bubba, unaware that a flirtation had been going on between Pepper and Stella for some time, now stood between the two of them after Stella returned from speaking with Chatty, outside. They were all waiting for McCager's opinion. Pepper was heartsick and told himself that he probably deserved this for all the heartbreaks he had caused, both knowingly and unknowingly. Stella was uncomfortable but tried, awkwardly, to get a conversation started with Pepper and not ignore him completely.

She leaned forward, across Bubba, and asked, "Did they teach you this when you trained to be a marshal?" Stella forced a smile.

Pepper, still cool to her, replied, "No, but I can have a shoot-out with the best of them."

"I forgit that you're a marshal," Bubba said, grinning. "You just blend in with all of us. Don't he, Stella?"

She forced another smile, "Yes, he does. Of course, the Burnetts, Chatty, and I have known him awhile now."

"Oh, yes. In fact, Pepper and Stella have dinner quite often down on the island."

Stella turned and glared, meant as a warning, at Chatty who was watching things unfold from beside Big Black's stall. But Chatty only smiled, mischievously. He was not about to be stopped. Of course, his first loyalty was always to Stella. But he didn't want her ending up with a mountain boy who spoke an Appalachian language and who, most assuredly, had never heard of Eudora Welty or William Faulkner.

Stella glanced sideways to see a pleased look on Pepper's face—and a furrow of concern on Bubba's. Then, before Stella could speak, Chatty continued, "Just last Sunday, we all went to the late service at the Presbyterian church. When I'm at my Buckhead home, which is just two houses down from the Governor's, I oversee senior bingo every Thursday night." He stopped and tried to summon forth some humility, but the truth is that humility and Chatty are strangers. "They count on me so." He paused and opened his mouth to speak again, but Stella beat him.

"Chatty, you should come over and see what the Governor's doing. Besides being educational, it will give you something to report to Mona Windsor. You know how she is. Give her a scoop and she'll pass over you when gossip comes creeping into her ear. *About you.*" Stella smiled like a saint.

"In theory, I can see where that would work, Stellie. But when you created that scene at the country club, she dined out on that for months. It was like when Princess Diana died. Everyone was looking for a new angle on her death." Stella stared, stone-faced, at Chatty. "When the regrettable scene happened at the country club which, you have to admit, *you started*, Mona spent days on the phone interviewing everyone who had been there and seen it." Chatty smiled again as Big Black nuzzled his cheek. "Of course, I was loyal to my beloved Stella." He stood straight, pulled his shoulders back and lifted his head with the perfect patrician nose. "I said not a word. Not a word."

Bubba, puzzled and completely confounded, looked over at Stella. "What's he talkin' about?"

"A bunch of foolishness," she responded, pushing a strand of red hair from her face. "It's a long story. I'll tell you another time."

Pepper leaned back, behind Bubba and Stella, and winked at Chatty who was all too proud of himself. Chatty smiled and winked back.

To spite them both, because she knew what was going on between Pepper and Chatty, Stella slipped her arm through Bubba's and laid her head on his shoulder. Bubba then pulled away his arm and put it around Stella, pulling her even closer. The faces of both Chatty and Pepper melted into a mixture of disappointment and dismay.

Chatty had nothing against Bubba, necessarily. He had been nice to him and helped him with the

Christmas decorations when they were the only two in the barn. He had even driven in some nails. But, let's be frank, Chatty told himself, his beautiful Stella Bankwell could not marry a boy named Bubba. Oh, no. That would almost be worse than the country club fiasco. By this point, Pepper had become almost family to the Burnetts and Chatty. What was Stella thinking?

While Chatty continued studying on what he could do to interfere, McCager called out, "Bubba!" loud enough that it startled both Chatty and his new love, Big Black.

"Yes, sir," Bubba replied.

"Buddy, you're right. The right hoof is turned under. My hand's too big that I'm havin' trouble turning it straight. Come here and see."

After picking up a glove from the table, Bubba stepped into the stall with McCager. This left Stella standing next to Pepper with no one between them. So, she summoned her courage.

"Pepper, I'm so happy you joined us for Christmas." Stella smiled at Pepper and he smiled back, in return. But as his grandpa' used to say, Pepper was "a stubborn old cuss." He wasn't letting Stella off the hook that easy. Of course, if she had been hooked by Bubba, there was no letting her off the hook, anyway.

"It's been quite an adventure. Not at all what I was expecting," Pepper said coolly.

"Yes, but as usual, you were the hero," Stella said, sincerely. And Pepper Culpepper knew there was no sarcasm there. But before he could speak, McCager walked out of the stall, pulling off his glove.

"That feels like a big foal. Somehow, we've got to get that hoof straightened. There's no coming out unless we do." He looked at Stella. "Any idea how things are goin' at the house?"

"None since I got back from supper."

"I think I'll mosey up and check on things," he replied. Realizing she would be left with Pepper—who she could see didn't think very much of her right now—Stella offered, "Governor, let me run up there. I need to use the powder room, anyway."

Flashlight in hand, Stella headed out of the barn where she looked up and now saw a full moon, shining down welcomed light which, of course, was made to seem all the brighter with the freshly-fallen snow.

Back at the kitchen table, she found Spencer filling out one of the crossword puzzles in a book her mama kept in the kitchen.

"How's it goin'?" she asked.

"Miss Bankwell, I'm finding that I'm beyond understanding many of these American crossword clues."

Stella laughed. "I'm American and I don't understand lots of the clues in that. What I meant is, how's it goin' in there?" Stella pointed to her mama's room down the hall.

Spencer shook his head. "There is much misery. Yet, as of now, no baby has arrived."

Stella sighed. "I'm going to the powder room then I'll stop in and see them."

Washing her hands, Stella looked in the mirror. Her hair had fallen around her face in a fetching manner after she had clipped it up. But, oh, she needed some lipstick. She'd grab a tube before going back to the barn. For a moment, as she viewed her reflection, she saw a country girl who was back where she belonged, and a thought streaked through her head: maybe she could come back and build a small English cottage on the farm somewhere. She could use her real estate license here. Or just enjoy a quiet life. She had enough money from her divorce settlement, so that was possible. The other night, when she couldn't sleep, she had watched Humphrey Bogart and Barbara Stanwyck in a movie called *The Two Mrs. Carrolls*. Part of it took place in a lovely English house with Tudor windows and beautiful gardens. Stella shook her head and, breaking out of her daydream, opened the door that led back to the real world.

She could hear Melissa half-crying, half-howling with pain. Stella stopped at her mama's bedroom and motioned her into the hall.

"How are things?"

"Hard, Stella Faye. She's been pushing nearly two hours. The doctor told Alva that if the baby isn't born soon, with her contractions still a minute apart and growing worse, then we really have something to fret about."

"I'm sure you're all doing the very best you can. I'll keep praying."

Her mama smiled and hugged Stella who then traipsed down the hall, taking a tube of lipstick from her.

She touched Spencer's shoulder as she passed. "See ya' later, Spencer."

"Miss Bankwell, before you go, what is a four letter world for three people, together?"

Stella's current predicament with Pepper and Bubba immediately came to mind.

"A crowd," Stella quipped, pushing open the door and going, leaving Spencer to lament, "but that's five letters."

Back at the barn, she found McCager and Bubba talking while Pepper stood nearby and listened.

"There she is," Bubba said, grinning ear-to-ear. He was ruggedly handsome while Pepper was more citified-handsome. Both men were about six feet one inch, their hair a different shade of sandy blonde, and both were blue-eyed.

I must have a type, she thought, disregarding the fact that Asher was dark-haired and looked more like Cary Grant.

"No baby, yet," she reported. "But she's trying."

"Same here," McCager said, looking grave.

"We can feel the curled-up hoof but it's tight quarters in there. We need someone with a small hand."

Stella didn't hesitate. "I'll give it a go. Let me put on a glove."

"I knew we could count on you," Bubba said grinning as he pumped his fist and Pepper turned away so no one could see him rolling his eyes.

Stella took off her ring and handed it to McCager. "I don't want to chance hurting her.

When Stella pulled on the glove, it hung loosely on her hand. The problem, noted McCager, was that when Stella finished and pulled her hand out, the glove was likely to be left in Sadie.

Everyone was silent for a moment before Stella said, "I'll exam her barehanded."

"Oh, Stella, dear, dear Stella," Chatty hugged her neck. "You're such a heroine." I'll stand right here and cheer you on!"

"You're going to watch?" Pepper asked, incredulously.

"Every moment." Chatty grinned from ear-to-ear.

Stella couldn't believe what she was hearing but was glad, nevertheless. Bubba opened the stall door. "Go get 'em, Red," and kissed her on the head. Chatty looked at Pepper and gave him a sad smile and a little shrug of his shoulders.

"I'll help keep her calm," Bubba promised, taking Sadie's halter and talking to her, soothingly.

McCager and Bubba then directed her to the curled hoof. "Okay," she said, "I feel it. Should I take the hoof and pull it out?"

"Yes," McCager and Bubba responded in unison.

"Alright, but if Sadie kicks me, just know I've already written my will." Stella grabbed onto the hoof in her mother's belly. It took a few tries but in a couple of minutes, she cried out, "I did it! The hoof's pointing just like the other!"

The group cheered for Stella and Cager stepped inside the stall, handing her a towel to clean her hand.

"I'm mighty proud of you," he said with a smile he reserved for special occasion.

Chatty was clapping his hands and dancing. "I knew my Stellie could do it!"

Soon, Bubba caught her up in a big hug and kissed her, again, on the top of the head.

Pepper, once more, was left the odd man out.

ꕤ

Back at the house, things weren't quite so cheerful. Miss Alva and Martha Annie were worried. Melissa was worn out from pushing, for over two hours, and with the end of another contraction, she fell back, against the pillow.

"That's it," she said. "I can't do this anymore."

"Yes, baby, you can. Please, don't give up." Another labor pain hit, and she let out a groan.

"C'mon. Push."

Fifteen minutes later and looking dangerously close to collapsing from pushing, Miss Martha Annie, who was standing at the foot of the bed, noticed a change.

"Miss Alva, come here."

When Miss Alva saw what Martha Annie had seen, she looked at Martha Annie who nodded, smiling. Pressing her hands together, she closed her eyes and said, "Thank you, Lord."

But Daniel was puzzled. "The baby is crowning," Martha Annie explained. "The top of the baby's head is showing." Miss Alva walked back to Melissa's side.

"Honey, your baby is really on its way. Just a little more pushing. Can you do that with the next contractions?"

Melissa smiled and nodded, then looked at Daniel for the strength to go on.

Martha Annie and Miss Alva had no doubt, and they began preparing things for the baby's arrival.

Chapter Nineteen

McCager Burnett always had a soft spot for Stella. He admired how she worked to help her parents put her through college, and how she quickly accelerated through the corporate ranks of a sports marketing company. Though he had had doubts when she first married Asher, he had high hopes that Stella was just what Asher needed to straighten up.

Asher's father, Jasper, was a fine man who turned a family fortune into incredible wealth. Asher was pretty much useless since he was always investing in stocks that went bankrupt. Finally, he became involved in a money laundering scheme, and would've gotten away with it, had Stella not convinced Pepper, McCager, and Chatty, the one who would save her life, into helping her. It put Asher, his girlfriend, Annabelle, and several others in federal prison for many years. Asher's thick, dark hair would be silver, perhaps white, before he was released.

Yes, as Chatty felt the need to share, Stella had made a scene at the Buckhead Country Club which kept Atlanta society talking for weeks. But when Stella uncovered the laundering scheme that recovered their money, she became society's most treasured member.

Stella, though she appreciated it, decided to settle instead on St. Simons Island—which led to her solving a murder mystery on nearby Sapelo Island.

Former Governor McCager Burnett loved Stella and Chatty as if they were his children. Chatty was a handful but Stella, with her great beauty and charm, was his favorite. Still, he couldn't be but surprised at what she'd just done. She was quite an admirable person.

Bubba picked up Stella, again, and whirled her around. She hugged his neck and kissed him on the cheek.

Now, Pepper had really gotten the message. Glumly, he thought, "What a Christmas this has turned out to be."

Sitting Stella back down, Bubba headed into the stall, joining McCager in checking on Fancy Sadie who seemed so much more calm.

"You saved the day. Again." Stella turned toward Pepper who smiled warmly, "Congratulations."

"Thank you," she responded, smiling in return. And further melting his heart.

As was his custom, Chatty interrupted and, with his hands on his hips, said, "Let's not forget who once risked his life to save Stella Faye Jackson," and pointed to himself. Suddenly a thought occurred to Pepper. Chatty was always pristinely dressed. But now? Pepper pulled out his phone and snapped a different kind of picture.

"Pepper Culpepper, if you share that photo, I shall be most upset." Holding out his hand to Pepper, "Please, allow me to view that photo. I, at least, want to ascertain that my pom-pom is fluffy and well-placed."

Staring at his photo, he said to Pepper, "You can do better. But just so long as it's only between friends, I'll allow it."

Pepper and Stella turned to each other and shook their heads—the first genuine moment they'd shared since Pepper arrived. It was a secret between them. Chatty always had to be perfect and, whenever possible, in charge. Now, they'd seen a completely different side of Chatty. And while Pepper was disappointed with how things were turning out with Stella, that perhaps she might really be lost to Bubba, Pepper could see that she had strong feelings for home. Sure, she'd solved mysteries and proven an unusually good fit into the island world. But the farm was a world away from St. Simons Island or Atlanta society.

Pepper smiled at her—"It's extraordinary how you so effortlessly step between such different worlds. First, you're a socialite, wearing designer clothes. Then, you slip easily into the casual, island life. And now, I see where you're most comfortable." Pepper looked at Stella for a few moments. "This is where you belong." Stella felt as though she should respond, but she didn't know what to say.

Then, "Stella, I've been thinking," Chatty announced as he approached. Stella just turned to her good friend with a tired look, "Yes, Chatty?"

"We're all in agreement as to the superb job I've done, decorating the barn which, undoubtedly, helped cheer Fancy Sadie and keep her spirits up during this ordeal."

"And your point is?" Stella raised an eyebrow and appraised his sock cap.

"I really feel the foal should be named after me."

Pepper groaned and Stella sighed. "Chatham, that will be Ronnie and Lynn's decision. These are registered horses with Big Black being a highly-bred animal. Normally, they combined the parents' names. Big Black is his nickname."

Chatty's face fell, and he pooched out his lower lip. "This is extraordinarily unfair."

"Everything is not about you, Chatty."

"It should be," Chatty said, sincerely. Of course, Pepper didn't try to hide his smile. He knew this was exactly what Chatty believed. At all times. In all places. Whether it was Atlanta's wealthiest neighborhood, Sea Island's exclusive community, his stunning plantation, or Stella's family's farm in the Appalachian foothills—the world was supposed to revolve around Chatty.

Before Stella could reply, Bubba called out, "The colt's on the way!" Stella ran back to the stall while Chatty ran in the opposite direction and Pepper sauntered over to watch. Sadie was lying down, and Big Black had his head stuck through the window.

"Oh, my gosh," Stella said, amazed by the sight. "She was really waiting for that hoof to be uncurled. And it won't be long now."

Suddenly, Stella turned on her heels and ran to the corner where Chatty, eyes wide, shoulders hunched, was chewing on his right thumbnail. Stella grabbed him by the elbow and said, "You're coming over here. You need to see this wonder of life."

"Oh, Stellie, please, don't make me go. I'm quite happy not knowing about the wonders of life."

With all her might, Stella started pulling Chatty toward the stall. But with all his might, he resisted.

"Pepper," she called. "Can you help me?"

"Don't call him," Chatty exclaimed with fright in his voice. "He'll make me go. It's not fair, two against one!"

Chatty's wailing was similar to Melissa's as Pepper helped Stella drag him to the stall where Pepper blocked his escape, warning, "And don't close your eyes."

"Please, watch? Do it for me," Stella pleaded.

"That's not fair, Stella. You know I'll do anything for you."

"Thank you," Stella said, then softly added, "Look."

Chatty opened his eyes and immediately, he was captivated by what he saw. He didn't care for the mess that came with it but he couldn't believe that a fully-formed creature could arrive so beautifully. McCager was holding the foal's head, with Bubba holding its legs, as it emerged. Completed exhausted now, the newborn lay in the hay.

"The baby is so far from his mama," Chatty pointed out.

"Don't worry," Stella's said. "She'll find her baby and clean it."

"Hey, Bubba," Pepper spoke up, asking, "What is it?"

"It's a colt!" he exclaimed.

Stella clapped, knowing that Lynn and Ronnie would be thrilled. Chatty looked unsure. "Does that mean it's a boy?" Stella nodded.

"But he hasn't stood up yet. Is he okay?"

"He's very weak," McCager said, standing up. "But in an hour or so, oh, you just wait and see. This little guy will be raring to run." Cager then came out of the stall, wiping his hands. "Well, Chatham, what did you think of that?"

It was obvious that a change, a new maturity, had come over Chatty. He put his hands on the sides of his face and said, "It's the most wondrous thing I've ever seen."

Pepper, standing beside Stella, unintentionally put his arm around her shoulders—while she, as natural as could be, put her arm around his waist, pulling him close.

And now, it was Bubba's turn to feel low and confused.

Unbeknownst to the joyous gang in the barn, Melissa, too, had produced some excitement and happiness of her own as Alva, never having been in this situation before, said to Martha Annie, "You'd best take over from here."

And in another fifteen minutes, a baby eased its way into Martha Annie's hands. "It's a boy!" she announced. Melissa wasn't wailing or moaning anymore, but crying tears of joy as she laughed, and Daniel kissed her. "Honey, you did great. I'm so proud of you."

Martha Annie laid the baby over her left arm and gave him a good smack on his backside which startled him breathing. And crying. Of course, by this time, everyone was crying. Next, Martha Annie laid the baby on the soft towel while Miss Alva took the scissors from the plastic bag and held them out for Daniel.

"Would you like to cut the cord?"

"Yes ma'am, where do I—?"

"Right here," she said as she pointed. "In a few days, the rest of it will dry up and fall off."

With that task accomplished, to the cheers of them all, the two women worked quickly to clean the baby, then laid him on Melissa's chest. The unbreakable bond, between mother and child, had begun.

"What did Dr. Colby say about feeding?" Martha Annie asked.

Her eyes flew open and she slapped her hand over her mouth. "I forgot he was on the phone." Picking up the receiver, Miss Alva gently wondered, "George, are you still there?"

"I am. And I heard everything. Y'all did quite well without me, I have to say." The doctor gave them a few more instructions, including how to help Melissa through feeding. "Tell her that he'll catch on. Even if it takes a little bit. Call me back, no matter how late, if y'all need me. I'll keep the phone close by."

After Alva and Martha Annie cleaned up, they said, "We're gonna take a walk out to barn and see if we have another new one out tonight." They wanted to give this new family some much-needed time together, alone.

It was bracing cold as they stepped out of the house, the snow making a resounding crunch as they walked. In less than two minutes, they were in the barn where Fancy Sadie had given birth just a few minutes earlier.

"What a beautiful colt," Martha Annie said. "Ronnie and Lynn are gonna be real pleased."

"Oh!" exclaimed Stella. "I need to call them but first, tell us about the baby."

When all was told from both sides, McCager Burnett said "I think we need to offer up a prayer of thanksgiving for this night of blessing." The group moved in a circle to hold hands where Stella found herself between Bubba and Pepper, holding the hand of each.

In his beautiful mountain voice and words, McCager said a lovely prayer finishing with "In our Savior's name, we pray. Amen."

And soon as he finished, he said, "What time is it?" He looked at his watch and smiled. "Thirty seconds before midnight and that means Christmas Day. "A baby boy born in the house and baby boy born in the stable. It's like something you'd see in a movie."

What no one knew was that, in the house, Spencer was serving hot tea made with water from the fireplace kettle and his special Christmas cookies he had made, to Daniel and Melissa. They had never seen such beautiful china before and never had they seen a silver tray.

In the barn, as the group still stood in the circle, Stella in a beautiful soprano, began to sing *Silent Night* and everyone joined in sincerely. Just as they finished, they heard munching in the fourth stall. "There's that raccoon," Cager said.

Only it wasn't.

It was a Jerusalem donkey with a black line down her back and another crossing her shoulder blades. It was a cross. A reminder of the donkey that carried Jesus into Jerusalem.

"Oh, my," said Stella, throwing her hand to her mouth. "Where did she come from?"

Bubba, putting his arm around her, said, "I'm guessin' from another farm. But it's quite a message, isn't it? If it's okay with Miss Martha Annie, when we find her owner, I'd like to buy her if they're of a mind of sellin' her, as a reminder of this incredible Christmas."

"I think that's a fine idea," said McCager. "Please, allow me and Miss Alva the pleasure to buy her as a gift to the Piney Wood Farm. Merry Christmas, y'all!

It was a Christmas Eve that no one who was there would ever forget the blessings, the snow blizzard, the babies born, and the Jerusalem donkey.

Epilogue

Two days later, Stella had her car packed and ready to go. She always hated saying goodbye to home but this time, Bubba made it even harder to leave. But soon, Stella was on her way to St. Simons Island. She'd decided to take the back roads. That way, she would have more time to think—about living on the island. Or, maybe, building a charming, little house in the shadow of her mountains. About Pepper who'd mentioned the possibility of a transfer. And Bubba who had complicated everything. She was deeply pondering so many things. Her phone had been ringing for a long while before Stella picked up.

"Hello," she answered. "What a nice surprise, hearing from you… Yes, Merry Christmas *and* Happy New Year… I'm doing well. And you? I figured you had some reason for calling… Did you say there was a murder? On Cumberland Island?"

Acknowledgments

My great-uncle, Oscar Cannon, and his wife, Fairy, who worked an almost 200-acre farm, introduced me to Turner's Corner, Mt. Pisgah (pronounced Pisgee in the mountains), Blood Mountain, the Appalachian trail, and the big black bear who had a job at the country store on the river, within eyesight of their yard. If you gave that bear a Coke, he danced merrily until he was ready for another. He refused Pepsi or Dr. Pepper. I was knee-high to my daddy when I saw how magical the lower Appalachians could be. To me and Stella Bankwell, they're still magical.

Many millions of people have been inspired by Dolly Parton, Appalachia's proudest daughter. I am grateful to the Lord that I have been personally touched by her talent and kindness. "We're soulmates and prayer mates," she wrote me recently. Yes, we are. This is how mountain people stick together. Trust me on this: you'd rather have Dolly pray for you than write a song for you. And, to Teresa, who has worked for Dolly for decades: she has shown us, this year, the power of

Almighty God and down-on-your-knees praying. My love to you two remarkable people.

There are many friends and family to appreciate but, please, allow me to thank my husband, John Tinker (Tink). I couldn't pull off these deadlines and all these stories without his love, encouragement, and advice. It's nice for a writer to be married to another writer. Especially, an Emmy award-winning one.

Finally, importantly, thank you, my readers and supporters. Without someone to read the words, mine would be a worthless effort.

The Author

Ronda Rich, whose Georgia family roots were planted around 1750, is the best-selling author of several books including *What Southern Women Know (That Every Woman Should)* and *The Town That Came A-Courtin'*, also a television movie. Her weekly syndicated column about Southern life appears in forty-seven newspapers across the Southeast.

Merry Chatty Christmas is the third Stella Bankwell story. *Saint Simons Island* was published in 2023, and *Sapelo Island* was published in 2024. *Cumberland Island* is the next mystery.

Learn more about her at www.rondarich.com.